"Don't you know those things aren't good for you?"

Anna nodded at the rich breakfast Miguel was making.

His head turned slightly and his gaze settled on her lips. "Lots of things aren't good for me."

Heat flared inside Anna like the instant spark of flint against steel. It seemed incredible that only a month ago she had thought she would never want another man. But standing by Miguel, she knew she was only just now learning what wanting a man was all about. Certainly she'd never felt this raw, aching attraction for her ex-fiancé. Or any man. Except Miguel. The idea was both exhilarating and frightening.

"Then why do you...indulge yourself?"

He grinned and looked away. Anna was relieved to find she could breathe again.

"A man only has a short time on this earth. To deny life's basic pleasures is foolish."

And Anna shivered at the thought of Miguel's pleasures.

Dear Reader,

You'll find the heartwarming themes of love and family in our November Romance novels. First up, longtime reader favorite Arlene James portrays *A Bride To Honor.* In this VIRGIN BRIDES title, a pretty party planner falls for a charming tycoon...whom another woman seeks to rope into a loveless marriage! But can honorable love prevail?

A little tyke takes a tumble, then awakes to ask a rough-hewn rancher, *Are You My Daddy?* So starts Leanna Wilson's poignant, emotional romance between a mom and a FABULOUS FATHER who "pretends" he's family. Karen Rose Smith finishes her enticing series DO YOU TAKE THIS STRANGER? with *Promises, Pumpkins and Prince Charming.* A wealthy bachelor lets a gun-shy single mom believe he's just a regular guy. Will their fairy-tale romance survive the truth?

FOLLOW THAT BABY, Silhouette's exciting cross-line continuity series, comes to Romance this month with *The Daddy and the Baby Doctor* by star author Kristin Morgan. An ex-soldier single dad butts heads with a beautiful pediatrician over a missing patient. Temperatures rise, pulses race—could marriage be the cure? It's said that opposites attract, and when *The Cowboy and the Debutante* cozy up on a rustic ranch...well, you'll just have to read this TWINS ON THE DOORSTEP title by Stella Bagwell to find out! A hairdresser dreams of becoming a *Lone Star Bride* when a handsome stranger passes through town. Don't miss the finale of Linda Varner's THREE WEDDINGS AND A FAMILY miniseries!

Beloved authors Lindsay Longford, Sandra Steffen, Susan Meier and Carolyn Zane return to our lineup next month, and in the new year we launch our brand-new promotion, FAMILY MATTERS. So keep coming back to Romance!

Happy Thanksgiving!

Mary-Theresa Hussey
Senior Editor, Silhouette Romance

Please address questions and book requests to:
Silhouette Reader Service
U.S.: 3010 Walden Ave., P.O. Box 1325, Buffalo, NY 14269
Canadian: P.O. Box 609, Fort Erie, Ont. L2A 5X3

STELLA Bagwell

THE COWBOY AND THE DEBUTANTE

Silhouette
ROMANCE™
Published by Silhouette Books
America's Publisher of Contemporary Romance

To Jason and Carmen,
may love be with you always.

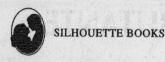

SILHOUETTE BOOKS

ISBN 0-373-19334-3

THE COWBOY AND THE DEBUTANTE

Copyright © 1998 by Stella Bagwell

This edition published by arrangement with Harlequin Books S.A.

® and TM are trademarks of Harlequin Books S.A., used under license. Trademarks indicated with ® are registered in the United States Patent and Trademark Office, the Canadian Trade Marks Office and in other countries.

Printed in U.S.A.

Books by Stella Bagwell

Silhouette Romance

Golden Glory #469
Moonlight Bandit #485
A Mist on the Mountain #510
Madeline's Song #543
The Outsider #560
The New Kid in Town #587
Cactus Rose #621
Hillbilly Heart #634
Teach Me #657
The White Night #674
No Horsing Around #699
That Southern Touch #723
Gentle as a Lamb #748
A Practical Man #789
Precious Pretender #812
Done to Perfection #836
Rodeo Rider #878
*Their First Thanksgiving #903
*The Best Christmas Ever #909
*New Year's Baby #915
Hero in Disguise #954
Corporate Cowgirl #991
Daniel's Daddy #1020
A Cowboy for Christmas #1052
Daddy Lessons #1085
Wanted: Wife #1140
†The Sheriff's Son #1218
†The Rancher's Bride #1224
†The Tycoon's Tots #1228
†The Rancher's Blessed Event #1296
†The Ranger and the Widow Woman #1314
†The Cowboy and the Debutante #1334

Silhouette Special Edition

Found: One Runaway Bride #1049

*Heartland Holidays Trilogy
†Twins on the Doorstep

STELLA BAGWELL

sold her first book to Silhouette in November 1985. Now, more than thirty novels later, she is still thrilled to see her books in print and can't imagine having any other job than that of writing about two people falling in love.

She lives in a small town in southeastern Oklahoma with her husband of twenty-six years. She has one son and daughter-in-law.

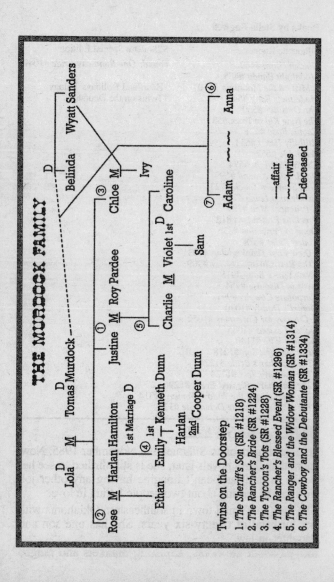

THE MURDOCK FAMILY

Lola $\underset{\text{M}}{\overset{\text{D}}{}}$ Tomas Murdock D Belinda D Wyatt Sanders

Rose $\underset{\text{M}}{}$ Harlan Hamilton
1st Marriage D

Justine $\underset{\text{M}}{\textcircled{1}}$ Roy Pardee   Chloe $\underset{\text{M}}{\textcircled{3}}$ Ivy

Ethan $\textcircled{2}$

Emily $\underset{\text{1st}}{\textcircled{4}}$ Kenneth Dunn

Harlan
2nd Cooper Dunn

Charlie $\underset{\text{M}}{\textcircled{5}}$ Violet 1st D Caroline

Sam

Adam $\textcircled{7}$ ～～～ Anna $\textcircled{6}$

—affair
～～twins
D–deceased

Twins on the Doorstep

Chapter One

Anna Murdock Sanders shook her finger at the nervous mare. "Ginger, I can see we need to have a girl-to-girl talk. That stallion is no good. He'll just take what he wants from you, then be on his merry way. Males are just naturally like that. Believe me, I know. That's why I'm swearing off men forever!"

Ignoring the warning, the mare nickered flirtingly at the stallion prancing around in the stall directly across from her.

A few feet farther down the long horse barn, Miguel Chavez stopped in his tracks as the young woman's words echoed back to him. He hadn't known anyone was in the stables, much less a woman who hated men!

Leaving the stall, he stepped into the alleyway and immediately spotted her lifting a saddle onto the paint's back. Tall and slender, she was dressed in black jeans and a moss green camp shirt. As she moved about the horse, adjusting blankets and latigo, copper curls danced like flames in the wind against the middle of her back.

She had to be his employer's daughter. Though Miguel had never seen her before, he'd heard Chloe and Wyatt Sanders speak of her. Anna and her twin brother, Adam, had been adopted as babies years ago by Chloe and Wyatt. Their actual birth parents had been Chloe's father and Wyatt's sister, both of whom had died shortly after the twins were born.

From what he'd heard, Anna was unlike her down-to-earth brother, who worked in the oil and gas businesses with his father. She was an accomplished pianist who'd spent the past few years traveling all over the States and abroad, playing concerts with big bands and symphony orchestras—a real debutante, who needed excitement, admiration and bright lights to make her happy.

The news that she was coming home hadn't reached Miguel. He didn't know why she was here, but he'd bet his last dollar it was because she wanted or needed something from her parents. Girls like her were always spoiled. He knew from firsthand experience.

Clearing his throat to warn her of his presence, Miguel moved down the alleyway toward her. Anna glanced up just as he came to a stop a few steps away.

"Hello," she said coolly as her eyes discreetly traveled up and down the lean length of the cowboy before her. He was dressed in jeans and chinks. Spurs with sunburst rowels were strapped to his black boots, and the sleeves of his heavy, brown cotton shirt were rolled up, exposing his thick forearms. Without a doubt, she'd never seen him before on the Bar M. He was a man not easily forgotten.

"Are you one of Mother's cowhands?" she asked forthrightly.

A wry twist to his mouth, he stepped forward and offered her his hand, then in a slight Mexican accent, he said, "I'm Miguel Chavez, the ranch foreman. And I don't think you've convinced Ginger that all men are bad," he said, inclining his head toward the mare. "She still appears to be interested."

As if to underscore his observation, Ginger once again nickered longingly at the stallion. Trying not to glower at the mare, Anna squared her shoulders and reluctantly reached to shake Miguel Chavez's hand. "She'll get past her infatuation."

Miguel raised his brows at her remark, but he said nothing. No doubt this woman had been infatuated many times. And gotten past it, he thought drily. With her looks she'd probably had men begging for the simple touch of her hand.

The repugnant idea had him quickly releasing her fingers, yet he still couldn't quite force his eyes to leave her face.

Her smooth ivory complexion told him she was young and also that she was vain enough not to let the bright sun ravage her luminous skin. Her full lips were dusky pink and slightly tilted at the corners. She had a straight patrician nose and pale green eyes that reminded Miguel of a spring aspen leaf. She wasn't exactly the most gorgeous woman he'd ever seen, but she possessed an earthy, sultriness about her that made the man in him want to keep looking. However, the cool expression in her eyes assured him she was not a woman for the taking. By him. Or any man.

Anna's auburn brows lifted quizzically as she

watched the cynical twist to his lips deepen. She didn't know what the man was thinking. But if it was about her, she certainly didn't like the idea that he found her amusing.

"I didn't realize mother had hired a new foreman," she admitted.

"I've been working on the Bar M for nearly a year now," he told her.

Pink color bathed her high cheekbones and she hated herself for letting him see her discomfiture. "Other than the holidays, I haven't spent too much time at home these past few months."

Anna hadn't deliberately planned it that way. One booking after another had kept her constantly on the road, and she'd been forced to postpone her trips home to a later date. And then, in the midst of all her work, she'd become involved with Scott and she supposed she'd gotten a little crazy after that. More than a little crazy, she thought with a megadose of self-deprecation. Thank goodness she'd gotten over him and canceled the wedding before her father had wasted an exorbitant amount of money on the ceremony...and she'd wasted herself on a man who had never really loved her.

"I don't need explanations, Miss Sanders," Miguel replied. "I didn't expect you to know me. I'm just the foreman around here."

Was he being impertinent or sincere? Anna's eyes scanned his dark face beneath the brim of his straw hat. She couldn't quite gauge his age, but she suspected he was somewhere near thirty-five. His face was lean and angular and had that hard-edged look that assured her his boyish days had long since passed.

His nose was hawkish, his chin slightly dented. His eyes were a deep hazel, full of green and brown flecks that glinted beneath thick black lashes. Yet it was his lips that drew Anna's full attention. The top one was thin and cruel looking while the bottom was full and sensual. It was a hard, masculine mouth and for some illogical reason Anna wondered how many women it had kissed.

Drawing in a deep, needy breath, she glanced away from him and turned back to the mare she'd been saddling. This wasn't like her, she thought wildly. She didn't look at any man and think the things she'd just been thinking.

"Call me Anna," she said curtly. "I'm sure you call my mother Chloe. She doesn't want anyone to be formal with her. And when I'm here at home, neither do I."

But when she was out among her fellow musicians, dazzling the crowd, she expected and demanded to be addressed formally. She hadn't come out and said as much, but Miguel could read the unspoken words very clearly. "Then you must be far more accustomed to being called Miss Sanders."

She couldn't stop the parting of her lips or the flare of her nostrils. "Are you always this impertinent?"

So she wasn't made of pure ice, Miguel decided as his gaze took its time studying her face. "I wasn't being impertinent. Just stating the obvious. You're hardly ever home. Otherwise you would have known about me. And I, you."

Shaking her thick red mane away from her face, she said, "You seem awfully sure of yourself, Mr. Chavez."

He shrugged, then grinned goadingly at her. Her spine immediately stiffened, and she glanced away from him.

"Are you thinking about getting me fired?"

Her head swung back around and she stared at him in surprise. "I don't interfere in my mother's business! She obviously wants you around here. So you must be good for something."

If Anna had been any other woman, Miguel would have already put her in her place. But she was Wyatt and Chloe's daughter and because they were such kind, wonderful people, he would not hurt them in such a way. Besides, Anna was from a whole different world than his. For his own sake, he needed to overlook her attitude.

"Oh, you might be surprised at the things I'm good at, Miss Sanders."

She turned away from him, but not before Miguel could see her lips compress to a thin line. No doubt she thought him vulgar and disgusting, but that was all right, too. He could make it just fine without women like Anna Sanders. And maybe it would be better for both of them if she understood that right now.

"Are you planning to stay long on the Bar M?"

She didn't answer immediately and Miguel watched her adjust the throat latch on the bridle. Like her mother, she had small hands. They moved with graceful dexterity and he could easily imagine them dancing over a set of ivory keys or a man's chest. The latter he tried not to dwell on.

She glanced over her shoulder at him and Miguel was intrigued by the knowing tilt to her lips. "I'm not sure yet. It depends on my job. Six weeks perhaps," she said.

"Then you're not...home to stay?"

Miguel didn't know why he'd asked the question, but he was irritated at himself because he had. Hell, it didn't matter how long the woman was going to be here. If he never saw her again after this moment he would survive just fine.

Home to stay. Miguel Chavez had no idea how wonderful those words sounded to Anna. She'd had years of extensive training in piano, and her parents and the rest of her family were proud of her accomplishments. They would surely be disappointed if she suddenly turned her back on her career.

"No. Only for an extended vacation," she said bluntly. Then, realizing the saddling was finished and there was no need for her to tarry here in the stables any longer, she led the mare ahead three or four steps and swung herself into the saddle.

Miguel stepped back out of the way and gave her a little salute from the brim of his hat. "*Adios,* Anna. Maybe before your vacation is over you'll have Ginger convinced to swear off the male gender, too."

Pausing, she looked down at him from her lofty perch and hoped he couldn't spot the faint pink on her cheeks. She couldn't remember the last time anyone or anything had made her blush. This man had managed to do it twice in less than five minutes. Damn him!

"If Ginger is as smart as I think she is, I'll have her turning her nose up at that stallion over there."

"Poor Ginger."

To Anna's amazement, she wanted to climb down

from the mare, poke her finger in the middle of Miguel Chavez's chest and tell him exactly what she thought of his raw remark. But she wouldn't give him the satisfaction of letting him know he riled her. For years Anna had trained herself to be a cool, sophisticated woman. It was an image she projected to her audience and even her family. She wasn't about to let this man know he could make her lose control.

"Goodbye, Mr. Chavez," she said bluntly, then touched her heels to the horse's sides and left him and the cool, dim interior of the stables behind.

She rode south, forging across the shallow Hondo, then up into the mountains where the pines grew thick and the carpet of needles beneath them silenced the mare's hooves.

At a rocky ledge halfway up, she reined Ginger to a halt and gazed back down on the valley below.

To Anna there was no place like the Hondo Valley. Santa Fe, where she'd played her last engagement, was known for its art and culture and mysticism, but this was the New Mexico Anna loved. There was everything in the valley. Horses, cattle, fruit orchards, forest and desert and something mixed of the two. And it was home. Nothing was better than that.

Ginger shook her head as a mosquito buzzed around her ears. Anna swatted the insect away, then patted the mare's neck. As she did, the lean, dark image of Miguel Chavez skipped through her mind.

The man had been a complete surprise to her. Not that having a Mexican-American working on the Bar M was anything unusual. Quite the contrary. Her parents normally hired more Hispanics than Anglos and they were as much a part of this area as the Apaches.

When she'd looked into his handsome face, his ancestry had been the last thing on her mind.

There was something about Miguel that had made her feel different in a way she'd never quite felt before. When he'd looked at her and grinned that outlandishly sexy grin at her, all she'd been able to think was that she was a woman and he was a man. It was ridiculous!

But Anna had far more important things to think about than a tough cowboy who was at least ten years older than her and probably married, besides. She had to gather herself together, refuel her mind and her body. Otherwise, after these next six weeks passed, she didn't know whether she could make herself go back on the road again.

She loved playing the piano, but she was growing weary of the nomadic life and the demands of performing for an audience. The weight of her job was taking a toll on her body. She couldn't remember the last time she'd slept the whole night through. Fatigue was her constant companion and her once-healthy appetite had almost vanished.

To please her parents last week, she'd gone for a medical checkup. When the doctor had assured Anna there was nothing physically wrong, both her mother and father had quickly assumed she was still grieving over her breakup with Scott. And Anna had found it easier to let them go on thinking she was simply suffering from a broken heart.

Truth was after she'd gotten over the initial shock of walking in and finding Scott in another woman's arms, Anna had come to realize she had never loved him with the same wild, deep need that her mother and father felt for each other. She hadn't been devastated when their relationship ended. She'd been relieved. And that in itself worried her. She was beginning to fear she was going to be like her birth mother, who'd flitted from one man and one bad relationship to the next.

With a heavy sigh, Anna reined the paint away from the ledge and headed her back down the mountain. The sun was dipping lower in the west, and her father would soon be home for supper. For his sake she was going to change clothes, put on her cheeriest face and make herself eat a whole plate of food.

Back at the stables there was no sign of Miguel Chavez. Although there were several wranglers working around the ranch yard doing last-minute evening chores, she unsaddled her mount, then brushed and fed her herself. The last thing she wanted was for word to get back to the foreman that she was a spoiled little rich girl. In her opinion the man was already far too smug. She didn't want to give him reason to be even more so.

Later that evening after supper, Anna helped her mother clear away the dirty dishes, then Chloe carried a pot of coffee out to the courtyard at the back of the ranch house where redwood furniture was grouped beneath a stand of piñon pines.

Her father had taken about two sips when his pager beeped. Mumbling his annoyance, he checked the number, then rose to his feet. "Looks like I'm going to have to leave you two beautiful ladies. Sander's Gas Exploration is calling."

"We'll try to do without you for a few minutes, darling," Chloe told him.

Anna watched her father head back into the house, then with a little sigh, snuggled deeper into the cushioned chair.

"Are you cold, honey? Would you rather go back in?" Chloe asked her.

Cooler air had moved in with the night, but Anna had pulled on a sweater before she'd left the house. "No. I'm fine. It's beautiful out tonight."

A few feet away an oval swimming pool was edged with huge terra-cotta pots filled with geraniums, marigolds and zinnias. Anna wished the water was warm enough to dive into. She couldn't remember when she'd taken the time for a leisurely swim. She couldn't remember the last time she'd gone at anything in a leisurely way.

A few feet away, Anna's mother, Chloe, studied her daughter's quiet profile for several moments, then said, "I wish you were enjoying yourself more. You've been back on the ranch for three days now, and I don't think I've heard you laugh yet."

Anna twisted her head around to face her mother. "I'm enjoying myself, Mother. You know how long I've wanted to come home."

Chloe didn't look a bit convinced. "Yes. But now that you're here I'm not so sure it's what you were really needing."

Grimacing, Anna rose from the chair and strolled over to the swimming pool. "Mother, please don't tell me I'd be happier if I were out looking for a man. Men are off-limits!"

Chloe laughed, then just as quickly apologized. "I'm sorry, honey, I'm not laughing at you. I realize you're miserable, but to hear you say your love life has ended is...ridiculous.''

Kneeling down near the edge of the pool, Anna trailed her fingers through the clear water. Just as she expected, it was still freezing. ''I mean what I said earlier, Mother. I'm swearing off men. This last thing with Scott proved to me that they're not to be trusted.''

She walked back over to where her mother sat stretched out on a chaise lounge, studying her with troubled eyes. ''Believe me, Anna, I felt just as you did before I met your father. You haven't forgotten that a man left me after we'd already planned to get married.''

Anna hadn't forgotten the story Chloe had related to her years before. ''I remember. You told him you couldn't bear children and he ran out on you. How could you have wanted to marry a piece of scum like that?''

Chloe chuckled. ''I could ask you the same thing about Scott? Why fret over someone who isn't worth it?''

Sighing again, Anna lifted her eyes to the sky. The night was clear, and stars blazed by the millions over the mountains. Deep in her heart Anna was beginning to think this was where she really belonged, not in some civic center a thousand miles away.

''Believe me, Mother, Scott opened my eyes. If it wasn't for seeing how much you and Daddy adore each other, I think I'd quit believing in love altogether.''

''Anna! You're just angry now. Besides, what about your aunts, Rose and Justine? They've both had long, wonderful marriages. And now your cousins Emily and Charlie are both happily married.''

Chloe was right. Most of her relatives had been lucky in love. But her mother hadn't mentioned Anna's birth parents, Belinda and Tomas. The two of them had been terribly unlucky. In fact, Belinda had more or less died from a broken heart and so had Tomas. But Anna loved Chloe too much to bring up that painful part of their lives.

"Mother...I think it's time I told you...I haven't been totally honest with you and Dad."

Chloe's brow arched with surprise. "What do you mean? About you and Scott?" Before Anna could respond, the older woman's mouth parted as another thought struck her. "Are you pregnant, darling? Is that why you're not eating? If you're worried—"

Anna quickly shook her head before her mother's assumption got out of hand. "No. I'm not pregnant. Scott and I never...well, I guess deep down, something kept telling me not to sleep with him. But as for a baby, I would love to have a child. Just not by Scott. I'd at least want to respect the father."

Chloe frowned with bewilderment. "If you're not pregnant, then what—"

"I'm talking about me being so...so melancholy. I'm not grieving over my ended relationship with Scott. That's all over and done with. I'm just overworked."

The tense expression on Chloe's face eased. "Of course you are, honey. That's why you're here on vacation. So you can rest and recuperate. And you will. You've only just gotten here. Give yourself time."

Anna sighed. "I'm not so sure I want to go back,

Mother. I'm not so sure I want to keep playing the piano professionally.''

Several moments passed in silence. Then, just as Anna was expecting her mother to burst out with shocked dismay, Chloe gentle smiled.

''Why haven't you said anything about this before?''

''Because I didn't want to upset you and Dad. I knew you would think I was losing my mind if I did.''

Chloe shook her head. ''Anna, you must live your own life as you want to live it. Not as you think we want you to.''

Of course Anna should have expected her mother would say those words. And so would her father. They would hide their disappointment just to make their daughter happy.

''You would say that,'' Anna mumbled.

''Since when have I or your father ever lied to you?''

Anna shook her head. ''Not any time that I can ever remember. But I know how much you've always wanted my career to go forward.''

''And it has,'' Chloe agreed. ''You've been making a great salary, you've traveled all over the world and seen all sorts of sights. But if your job is making you unhappy…then you need to stop and ask yourself what it is you really want.''

Anna went over to her mother's chair, knelt down at the arm and pressed her hand over her mother's. ''I have been, Mother. And I think I fell in with Scott's plans to get married not so much because I loved him or even needed him, but because I wanted children and a home and I thought he could give those things to me.''

Chloe's gentle smile was understanding. ''And you want those things more than you want to travel and play the piano.''

Anna's head bobbed up and down. ''Does that sound crazy?''

Chloe laughed softly, then reached over and patted her daughter's cheek. ''If it does then I've been crazy for the past twenty-five years.''

She hadn't really meant to blurt all of this out to her mother this evening, but she felt a bit better for it.

Rising to her feet, Anna said, ''Well, it does sound crazy, actually. A woman needs a man to have a home and children. And since I don't want a man in my life, I've got to turn my attention to other things.''

''What other things?''

Anna's slender shoulders lifted then fell. ''I don't know. Maybe I should just throw myself back into the music and forget about the children and the white picket fence. Maybe after six weeks of rest I'll be itching to perform again.'' A wan smile tilted her lips. ''In the meantime, I'm simply going to enjoy being home. It was such a pleasure to ride Ginger this afternoon. Just being with the horses again is therapeutic for me.''

''I'm glad.''

Her lips suddenly thinned to a smirk. ''By the way, I met your new foreman earlier before I went out riding. I didn't realize Lester had left.''

Chloe nodded. ''Lester had reached retirement age and he and his wife wanted to do some traveling.''

Lester had been on the Bar M for twenty years. He

was a bowlegged, raw-boned, pipe smoker who'd rarely shown the top of his bald head to anyone. He'd been more or less like a grandpa to Anna and Adam and their younger sister, Ivy. Miguel Chavez was nothing like Lester.

"Where did you find Mr. Chavez?"

"Your uncle Roy knew him. Miguel lived in Carrizozo for several years. Before that, Albuquerque, I think. What did you think of him?"

Anna had thought far too many things. In fact, she was still wondering why that idiotic thought about his mouth had ever entered her head.

"Well, I'm sure he's a strong, capable man or you wouldn't have him here."

A knowing little smile on her face, Chloe said, "Miguel is a good man, but he doesn't profess to know all that much about racehorses. He sees to the cattle end of things and makes sure the cowhands do all the rough stable work for me."

Anna's brows lifted. Miguel Chavez possessed more than a striking appearance. Self-confidence oozed from every pore on the man. "He doesn't know about horses? I don't believe that for a minute."

Chloe rose from the chaise lounge and stretched. "Well, of course he knows about horses. He rides like a man who was born in the saddle. But I'm talking about the ins and outs of racing."

Anna glanced at her as another question struck her. "Is he...Miguel living in the old foreman's house?"

The place she referred to was a midsize log structure built almost a mile south of the ranch house and halfway up the mountain. Anna had always been fond of the homestead. It was quiet and secluded and had a spectacular view of Sierra Blanca to the west.

Chloe nodded, then with an assessing gleam in her eye, added, "And he's single. I think he was married years ago. I don't know what happened. Apparently some woman dealt him some misery. I suppose, like you, he's sworn off the opposite sex. Since he's been here I haven't seen him look sideways at one, much less have one to his house as a date."

For some reason, Anna didn't feel comfortable talking about Miguel Chavez's personal life. He'd seemed a private person, one who kept his deeper thoughts to himself. She respected that, and anyway, it was no concern of hers whether the man was single or married or a masochist. She had her own problems to deal with.

"I'm sure he has his reasons," Anna said, though she couldn't help wondering if some woman had left him emotionally bruised and beaten. She sincerely doubted it. Miguel Chavez seemed too tough to have ever suffered a broken heart.

"Yes, I'm sure he's had his reasons," her mother said with a sigh. "But it seems such a shame. No one should be that alone."

Her mother spoke with the same sort of fretfulness she might have used if she were talking about Adam, but that didn't surprise Anna. Chloe wanted everyone she knew to be as happy as her. And in her mother's eyes, love and happiness were synonymous.

"Maybe Miguel Chavez simply prefers his own company," Anna said, then, looping her arm around her mother's, she urged the other woman toward the house. "Let's go in. The breeze is getting downright cold."

"Wait a minute, darling, the coffeepot." She walked over to a small table and picked up the insulated container, then rejoined her daughter. "Now back to Miguel—he doesn't know what he prefers. He's lived alone for so long, he's forgotten what female companionship is all about."

Chloe's candor brought a pink flush to Anna's cheeks. "Mother, I imagine Miguel Chavez has already forgotten more about women than the average man would know in a lifetime."

Suddenly Chloe began to laugh, and Anna glanced at her sharply as the two of them entered the back door of the kitchen.

"You find that funny?"

Chloe's laughter quickly sobered but a wide smile remained on her face. "No, dear. I'm just happy you noticed."

Chapter Two

Early the next morning, Anna sat up in bed and pushed her long tousled hair away from her face. Birds were singing, and through the open blinds of a nearby window, she could see the gray light of dawn casting soft shadows across the courtyard beyond her bedroom. Her mother would already be at the stables. From the time Chloe had been old enough to follow Tomas Murdock on two sturdy legs, she had learned the rule of feeding the horses before herself.

The thought put a wry smile on Anna's lips. Chloe's reputation as a horse breeder and trainer didn't stop at Lincoln County or even the state of New Mexico. People from as far as Louisiana, Arkansas and Kentucky had come to buy her yearlings.

Anna was very proud of her mother. She was equally as proud of her father, who was well-known in the gas and oil business. And now her brother, Adam, was making a name for himself as an oilman, too. Then there was her little sister, Ivy, who was studying hard to become a doctor. Each member of the family had a successful field they enjoyed working in. Anna would be the only quitter in the bunch if she turned her back on her musical career.

But she didn't want to spoil the morning by dwelling on such deep thoughts. And anyway, she wasn't going to be practicing piano today or listening to her road manager map out the next week's agenda, she was going to help her mother in the stables and that was enough to lift her spirits.

By seven-thirty breakfast was over, and Anna accompanied her mother to the stables. Much to her chagrin, the first thing she saw when she entered the huge building was Miguel Chavez. He was dressed much the same as yesterday only a pair of batwing chaps had replaced the shorter chinks and rather than the straw, a brown felt hat was riding low on his forehead.

In spite of Anna's vow to ignore the male gender, she couldn't help but be struck by the man's looks. He had something more than just pleasant features. There was a sensuousness about him, a blatant masculinity that made her very aware of his dark hair and skin, his broad shoulders, lean hips and long strong legs. And as she and her mother drew closer, Anna's heart raced with foolish anticipation. Of what, she didn't know. She only knew this man struck some sort of chord in her that she hadn't even known she possessed.

"Good morning, Miguel," Chloe greeted him warmly.

He turned from the horse he was saddling and nodded in greeting. "Good morning, Chloe, Anna."

"I see you're taking Rimrock out today," Chloe remarked. "How's his ankle?"

"The swelling is down and he's had a rest for the past couple of days, so I thought I would use him today and see what happens."

"Are you starting roundup this morning or later this week?" Chloe asked him. "I know you wanted to have everything else caught up before you began."

Miguel inclined his head. "This morning is the beginning," he answered. "I expect the job will take at least a week."

Chloe glanced suggestively at Anna. "Darling, why don't you saddle Ginger and ride along with Miguel? I'm sure he'd be glad for the extra help, and I know how much you always enjoyed roundup."

Anna's mouth popped open. Ride along with Miguel?

"Mother! Miguel doesn't want to be bothered. The man has work to do."

Chloe grimaced at her, then turned back to her foreman. "Miguel, I assure you Anna is a first-rate cowgirl. Since she started her music career, she hasn't done much of it, but she can probably outrope and outride half the cowboys you'll be using today."

Miguel's brows arched ever so slightly as his hazel eyes skittered up and down Anna's slender figure. She was wearing black jeans and matching jacket. Beneath its opening he could see a pale pink knit shirt that clung to her breasts like an eager hand. She looked anything but a cowgirl. "Is that true, Anna?"

The way he said her name with just the faintest bit of accent made a tiny shiver race down her spine. Her gaze drifting to a pearl snap in the middle of his chest, she said, "I'm sure you know mothers are biased."

Chloe rolled her eyes and tapped the toe of her boot. "Miguel knows I don't exaggerate. But if you'd rather not go, you can stay here and help me groom a few of the yearlings."

Groom the yearlings? Anna could already picture herself being pawed and bitten and rope-burned. Yearlings didn't take to being spruced up, especially when it came to using clippers around their ears and nose and feet.

She was already wearing a heavy, lined jean jacket to protect her against the early-morning coolness, and she could find a pair of chaps in the tack room. Anything else she might need would be on the chuck wagon.

"No. I think I'll saddle Ginger and head out to the roundup." She glanced at Miguel who was still studying her with faint skepticism. "But you don't have to wait for me, Miguel. Just tell me the area where you'll be and I'll catch up."

"There's no hurry. I have a few things to take care of here at the ranch yard before I leave. I'll find you when I'm ready."

To keep insisting he go on without her would be rude, Anna decided. And it was obvious he was going out of his way to please her mother. Oh, Lord, what was she letting herself in for? she wondered.

"Fine. It won't take me long to saddle Ginger," she told him.

Chloe chuckled softly as the two women headed on down the alleyway between the two endless rows of horse stalls. "I figured once I said 'groom the yearlings' you'd decide pretty quick you wanted to head out on the roundup.''

"Mother!" Anna hissed under her breath, even though they were clearly out of Miguel's earshot. "Why did you do that to me?"

Chloe shot her daughter an innocent look. "Do what, honey?"

Anna groaned. "You know what! You practically threw me at that man! Mother, he isn't Lester!"

"No. He certainly isn't. He's far younger and a lot better looking, don't you think?"

Sighing, Anna shook her head with disbelief. "If you're trying to do a bit of matchmaking here, Mother, you need to open your eyes and see Miguel Chavez is at least ten years older than me. Probably more."

Chloe's green eyes twinkled mischievously. "So what does age have to do with anything? Besides, I'm not doing any sort of matchmaking. Why would I be, when you keep insisting you're off men forever?"

The two of them had reached Ginger's stall. Anna reached for the nylon lead rope hanging on the outside of the door.

"Mother, you're being deliberately obtuse and you know it."

"Oh, Lord, Anna, you're being overly sensitive, aren't you? I merely thought you'd enjoy going on roundup today. It's your first week back home. I want you to loosen up and quit all this fretting about trivial things."

Trivial! Her reaction to Miguel Chavez was anything but trivial, Anna thought as she watched her mother's swinging stride carry her on to the tack room. But she would deal with it, she told herself fiercely.

She wasn't about to let the man ruin her much-needed vacation.

Twenty minutes later Anna was ready and waiting with her paint mare outside the horse barn. She'd found a pair of fringed chaps she used to wear during her teenaged days when she'd helped her mother gallop the racehorses. Anna had added on a bit of weight since that time, but she managed to zip the tan leather around her legs. Hopefully once she had them on for a while, the leather would stretch. In any case, she wouldn't ride in the brush without chaps. She knew from experience what a patch of prickly pear or choya cactus could do to a person's unprotected legs.

She was doing a few squats, trying to gain her legs a bit of breathing space when a male voice suddenly sounded behind her.

"Are you doing your morning aerobics or trying to teach Ginger a new trick?"

Gasping with surprise, Anna whirled around to see Miguel standing a few feet away, a sorrel quietly waiting beside his shoulder

"Oh!" Lifting her chin, she tugged at the hem of her jacket but it was far too short to hide anything. "I...uh, these are my old chaps and I've grown a little since I last had them on."

The grin on his face deepened, and Anna could feel her cheeks getting redder. This wasn't the way she wanted to start her day. She'd left one lecherous man behind. Yet here she was looking at another one as though he was the grandest thing to come along since sliced bread. She wished she could kick herself.

"You must have been a skinny little thing," he observed.

His eyes slid pointedly up and down the length of her, and Anna had never felt so stripped and naked in all her life. Which was crazy. She was covered with several layers of clothing!

Desperate to put a halt to the whole ridiculous encounter, Anna tossed the reins over Ginger's head and swung herself up and into the saddle.

"Don't worry. The wind won't blow me off if I gallop."

A nylon lariat was coiled around her saddle horn, and a slicker and saddle bags were tied to the skirt of the saddle. If she was a greenhorn she was doing a good job of faking it. Still, Miguel found it hard to believe the soft slender woman sitting astride the paint was little more than a flighty musician, a pampered debutante.

Whether Miss Anna Sanders was capable of being a cowgirl or not, Miguel would grit his teeth and put up with her today. For Chloe's sake. But tomorrow she'd be on her own. He was a ranch foreman, not a baby-sitter or social director.

"That's good to know, Anna. Hopefully we won't have to gallop."

Bemused, Anna watched him swing up into the sorrel's saddle. Was the man insulting her, teasing her, or was he actually serious? His smooth expression left her without a clue.

The two of them eased their mounts out of the ranch yard, past the last of the cattle pens, then east toward the river.

Anna said nothing as she rode stirrup to stirrup with Miguel Chavez. But her lack of conversation wasn't a personal affront to the man. When she was riding the range, she was always entranced by the sights and sounds around her. And it had been so long since she'd been out of doors, away from the pressures of her job.

"Your sister, Ivy, rarely rides whenever she's home. I don't believe she feels very safe around horses."

She glanced at him. "You've met Ivy?"

He nodded. "She's more like her father, I think."

Anna smiled briefly. "I expect so. Daddy never had an affinity for horseflesh."

"Your father is a very good man."

It pleased her to know this man appreciated her family. "Yes. Very."

The two of them crossed the stirrup-deep river, then headed toward the base of the mountain. As they rode, Anna stole glimpses of Miguel Chavez from the corner of her eye. He rose with the ease of a man long accustomed to the saddle, and as she covertly studied him, she couldn't help but think of all her mother had said about him yesterday.

He'd been married once. A long time ago. And he didn't date. Why? Anna wondered. It couldn't be for a lack of willing females. She suspected the man could crook his finger at most any woman, and she'd come running. Except herself, of course.

"Do you have a family, Miguel?"

"Not around here. My mother lives in Mexico. My father passed away several years ago."

He looked at her as though he found her questions intrusive, and Anna decided she would bite off her tongue before she asked him anything more.

"And I'm not married," he added. "Nor do I want to be. Surely your mother has already told you that."

Anna very nearly gasped at his remark. Did he actually think she was so desperately interested in him she'd resort to discussing him with her mother? She'd never encountered such arrogance.

Still, the bitter look on his face bothered her. She hadn't meant to pry into his private life. Nor was it a good idea to know all that much about the man. But she wanted to know, and that was the most disturbing part of it all.

Several long minutes passed without so much as a glance from her. Miguel's gaze fell to her left hand resting against her thigh. There was no ring of engagement or marriage. Though he didn't know exactly how old she was. He thought he'd remembered someone saying the twins were twenty-four or -five. Not that old as far as age goes, but certainly old enough to be married.

The idea put a dour look on Miguel's face. Women of Anna's status rarely needed or wanted a man around their neck. And when they did make the mistake of marrying, it always ended disastrously. When he'd first met Charlene, she'd been young and rich, just like Anna. And he'd been a hopeless fool to think he could keep her happy.

"You haven't gotten the urge to marry?"

She turned a shocked glare on him. "Who's been talking about me?"

Her odd reaction caused Miguel to study her for long moments. "I don't repeat or listen to gossip, Anna. I know nothing about your marital status. I was merely making conversation."

Embarrassed heat flooded her cheeks. Of course he couldn't know about Scott. No one except her parents knew her intended had turned to another woman before the wedding plans were completely finalized.

Staring straight ahead, she said flatly, "Well, for your information, I'm not married. I doubt I ever will be."

From the corner of her eye, Anna noticed he didn't appear a bit surprised by her grim announcement. But then, he'd overheard her opinion about men in the stables. Apparently he'd not forgotten her vow.

"I'm sure having a husband would be a hindrance to your life-style."

She stared at him, her features wrinkling with dismay. "A hindrance?"

Miguel quickly shook his head. "Forget it. We'd better kick our mounts up. The boys are probably waiting on me."

Miguel Chavez believed she was selfish. He obviously thought nothing mattered to her except living the high life. She could have very nearly laughed if the whole thing hadn't been so painful. From the time she'd been a small child Anna had never done what she really wanted. Even where Scott was concerned, she'd planned to make all sorts of sacrifices to ensure their marriage would start out on solid ground. But let Miguel think what he wanted. What she carried around in her heart was her own business.

In mutual consent, Anna touched her heels to Ginger's sides. Their horses immediately broke into a short lope and the faster gait put a halt to any more conversation. Anna was relieved. The man was like barbed wire. Every word, every glance from him pricked her in the most irritating way.

Within a few minutes they topped a rise. In the valley below, a group of portable cattle pens and a squeeze chute had been set up to make a working ranch yard. Six more cowboys and twice that many saddled horses were gathered around the orange metal fencing. Several yards beyond, a chuck wagon was parked and ready to prepare the noonday meal. Near to the makeshift kitchen, a fire had been built and a huge granite coffeepot hung over the low flames. As she and the foreman rode into camp, the scent of the strong brew mingled with horses and leather and crushed sagebrush. It was a mixture of smells Anna loved, and as she sniffed she was enveloped with fond memories.

Several years had passed since Anna had helped with spring roundup. Since then, Lester had retired, and now Miguel Chavez had stepped in to fill his boots. The fact that her mother had hired the man told Anna she obviously respected him as a person and, also, that he knew his business well. Anna normally trusted her mother's judgment, but this was one time she was anxious to see if the man lived up to his reputation.

From the moment Miguel had walked up on Anna last evening in the stables, he'd gotten the impression she was far too delicate and sensitive to deal with any sort of ranch work. She was a pianist, for heaven's sake. She entertained rich people. Riding the desert range and branding cattle might have been in Anna's life years ago, but it wasn't now.

Throughout the morning Miguel kept a close eye on her. After a couple hours passed, he had to concede, in spite of her hothouse looks, she wasn't helpless. She handled Ginger with practiced ease and had no problems heading rollicking calves down off the mountains and into the holding pens.

In fact, she worked with dogged persistence and appeared to know the lay of the land far better than any of the hands. Still Miguel wasn't ready to admit she belonged out here on roundup. Especially when the work on the ground started.

By the time the group stopped to eat a dinner of refried beans, Spanish rice and hot tortillas, more than three hundred head of calves had been gathered. After the meal was over, fires were built in one of the pens and branding irons in the shape of a bar resting atop an M were thrust into the hot coals to heat.

When Miguel realized Anna intended to help with this chore, too, he was shocked. As she made her way toward the work pens, he took her by the arm and led her a few yards out of earshot of the other cowboys.

"Don't tell me you have the notion you're going to join the men in the work pens," he said to her.

She arched one haughty brow at him. "Of course. That's why I came out here…to help with roundup."

Miguel should have expected her to argue with him. It was probably a rare thing for her to ever hear the word *no*. "Look, Anna, you're going to get smeared with manure and dirt. You might even get burned or kicked or worse."

She shot him a tired look. "Just because I've been living away for the past few years, doesn't mean I've forgotten anything about my upbringing, Miguel. Or are you afraid I'm going to be in the way of your cowboys?"

Miguel didn't exactly think she'd be in the way. He really didn't know why he was so opposed to her working on the ground. He only knew he felt a need to protect her.

Hell, Miguel, he silently cursed himself. You ought to know Anna doesn't need protecting. She was one of those women who prided herself on her independence and self-reliance. If she ever did need a man's strength or shoulder to rely on, it wouldn't be a Mexican cowboy like himself.

"No," he said with sudden gruffness. "I don't think you'll be in the way. I just thought I'd save you from the nasty work. But if that's your cup of tea, have at it."

He jerked his head toward the pens, where already the calves were bawling with loud protests, and the stench of burning hair and hide drifted on the high-desert wind.

It was obvious to Anna that he didn't want her working in the pens. She didn't know if his attitude stemmed from genuine concern for her safety or to simply be the boss. Either way it annoyed her. From the time she'd been old enough and strong enough to hold a kicking calf's hocks together, she'd helped her mother and Aunt Rose in the branding pen. She didn't appreciate an outsider telling her she was no longer welcome.

"Look, Miguel, the Bar M wasn't always blessed with as many hands as you have working here for you today. When my twin and I were born, my mother and aunts were taking care of this ranch by themselves. And even years later, when I was a small girl, it wasn't all that much better. I know how to work, and I'm not afraid of getting my hands dirty."

"Have you thought what would happen if you get

your hand or finger crushed or burned? Your career would end.''

Her expression grim, she said, "If need be, I can face my career ending. What I can't bear is being cloistered. Ever.''

He held his palms up as if to say he wasn't going to argue with her. "You want to be reckless, go right ahead. I won't stop you.''

Reckless. Anna wished for once she could let herself really go. Right at the moment she'd take immense pleasure in slapping Miguel Chavez's jaw. "But you'd like to stop me," she said crisply.

He let out a rough sigh. To deal with a precocious woman on today of all days was the last thing Miguel needed. "It doesn't matter what I want. This is your ranch. I'm sure you're going to do what pleases you, and to hell with my wishes.''

Anna gasped and was totally unaware that her fists had become planted on both her hips. "This isn't my ranch, either! It belongs to my parents and my aunts and uncles.''

He glanced pointedly away from her, and Anna realized he was annoyed that she was wasting his time with trivial facts. Well, wasn't that too bad, she thought. He was the one who'd started all this nonsense in the first place.

"Isn't that all the same?" he asked.

"No! And I don't like the impression I'm getting from you.''

His dark brows lifted skeptically. "What impression?''

"That you think I'm—some sort of little princess that has to be condescended to.''

His nostrils flared, and something dark and dangerous flickered in his hazel eyes. "If you think you can make me believe for one minute that you've ever had to suffer and struggle to make ends meet, you're sadly mistaken. I'm not a fool, Anna. You were born into wealth, and you wouldn't know what it was like to be without it."

He was so wrong that she didn't even want to try to correct his thinking. And where was his thinking coming from? It didn't matter, she told herself fiercely. What Miguel Chavez thought of her was his own problem.

"My mother said you were a good man. Obviously she doesn't know you."

Anna turned and stomped away from him. She went straight to the branding pen, climbed the metal fence and jumped to the ground inside. Let Miguel be put out with her, she thought angrily. She was home on vacation. If she wanted to help with roundup, she would.

An hour later sweat was pouring down her face, tracking the fine dust coating her skin. She'd long ago shed her jean jacket, and manure now stained the front of her pink cotton shirt and splotched her chaps. But none of those discomforts bothered Anna nearly as much as Miguel's earlier remarks had. She was still seething over his attitude, and though he'd been working only a few steps away from her, she'd done little more than grunt in his direction.

"You better watch out, Anna. This one is a strong cuss," the cowhand warned as he bulldogged the half-grown calf to the ground.

Someone appeared with a branding iron just as she

managed to grab the calf's two back legs. "I'm watching," Anna assured him, "just hurry and—"

Anna's next word never got past her lips. The next thing she knew the ground slammed against her back and bright white lights were floating in front of her eyes.

"Anna! Anna, can you hear me?"

The deep male voice persisted, demanding she wake up and open her eyes. Anna struggled to see through the cobwebs floating around in her head.

"Miguel? Is that you?" she asked weakly.

Cool, rough fingers touched her temple, and she realized something was wrong with her head. Pain was zinging through it like bolts of lightning.

"Yes. It's Miguel," the male voice answered.

A strong arm slid beneath her shoulders and pillowed her upper body in a half-sitting position. "What...happened?" she asked.

"You've been kicked," he said grimly. "Can you see me?"

Anna tried her best to focus her gaze on his dark face. Her vision was still blurred, but thankfully it was quickly clearing.

"Yes. Was I...kicked in the head?" She brought her fingers up to her forehead. It felt like someone had whammed her with a hammer.

"Right in the temple."

"She took a pretty good lick, boss," one of the cowboys that were grouped around them said. "Maybe she should go to the doctor."

"You're probably right, Jim," Miguel agreed. "Can you men go on, while I take Anna back to the ranch?"

"No!" Anna practically shouted and made a sudden move to get to her feet.

"Stay where you are!"

The demanding tone of Miguel's voice was like a shot of adrenaline to Anna. She shoved herself away from him and stood on rubbery legs.

"I'm okay. I don't need a doctor!"

Another cowhand retrieved her felt hat from the ground where she'd fallen and handed it to her. Anna jammed it back on her head and tried not to wince as it settled over the goose egg that had already formed beneath her scalp.

"You probably have a concussion," Miguel warned her.

"I can see, and I don't have the urge to throw up. I just have an ache in my head. And you would, too, under the circumstances."

Miguel motioned for the men to get back to work, then, taking Anna by the arm, he led her over to the back of the chuck wagon where the two of them would be out of sight from the others.

"Why are you continuing to argue with me? You were briefly knocked out cold!" he told her, his voice rough with frustration. "I want you to swallow a couple of pain pills, and then I'm going to ride with you back to the ranch."

"Why? I don't need to go back to the ranch."

He glared at her with angry disbelief, and Anna wished she had the strength to knock the know-it-all look off his face.

"You didn't need to be down in the branding pen, either," he said, "but you wouldn't listen to me."

"Oh, sure, throw that up to me! I'm sure it tickles you to death to be able to say 'I told you so.'"

At this very moment, Miguel wanted to shake her, then hold her as tightly as he could. He'd never been so frightened as when he'd heard the thud of the calf's hoof striking her head and then had seen her lying white-faced and lifeless on the ground.

"Nothing about this situation tickles me Anna."

She tried not to feel hurt by his attitude. After all, nowhere was it written that he had to like her. "In other words, you never wanted me around in the first place. You only tolerated my presence because of my mother. Well, if you must know, I only came out here on this roundup to please my mother."

"And here I thought all this time you were pining to be near me," he said sarcastically.

"You really are—" she shook her head "—sickening!"

Suddenly his hand was cupping the back of her neck and his face was dangerously close to hers. "What would you know about me, Anna Murdock Sanders? You've been away from this ranch for more than a year. You didn't even know your mother had hired a new man to run the place. I can plainly see who and what you care about!"

Anger turned her cheeks scarlet and made her head pound just that much worse. "I think your hands and your notions are both misguided," she said through gritted teeth.

Something flared in his eyes, but before Anna could figure out what it was, pressure from his fingers propelled her forward and a pair of hard lips clamped down on hers.

She groaned a protest in her throat, and her fists came up to push against his shoulders. But that was where her fight ended. Her stunned outrage was suddenly forgotten as her senses gave over to the overwhelming sensation of being in his arms, tasting his hard, warm lips.

Anna was certain an eternity had passed before he finally ended the kiss and looked down at her. By then her legs were trembling even worse than before, and her head reeled with pain and the humiliation of surrendering to the man.

"I'm certain," he muttered, "that you think entirely too much. As for my hands and my notions—you won't be bothered by either of them again!"

"That's the best news I've had in years!"

Miguel didn't know what in hell had come over him. He hadn't wanted to kiss Anna Murdock Sanders! But he had, and even now he still couldn't find the strength to put her away from him.

"Can you see straight now?" he asked coolly.

Her nostrils flared daintily as her eyes focused on the tantalizing curve of his lips. She was probably just one of many women that had tasted his mouth, she told herself. What had just transpired between them had meant nothing to him, except an act of punishment.

"Straighter than I've ever seen before!"

"Good. Then get on your horse and get out of here before I say or do something I'll really regret."

"Believe me, I already have."

She jerked away from him and strode around to the front of the chuck wagon. The cook searched out a bottle of painkillers for her and Anna quickly swallowed one down with a swig of bitter coffee. By the time she'd untethered Ginger and swung herself up into the saddle, Miguel had already dismissed her and gone back to work in the branding pen. Now all she had to do was ride three miles back to the ranch and try to forget she'd ever met the man!

Chapter Three

"Anna! Anna, wake up!"

This time it was her mother's instructions rather than Miguel's and the urgency in the older woman's voice caused Anna to come awake instantly.

"What's wrong?" She glanced at the clock on the nightstand and was alarmed to see it was the middle of the night.

"Don't panic, darling, but we've had a telephone call from South America. It sounds as though Adam has been involved in some sort of accident out at one of the oil sites."

Anna bolted upright in bed, and the sudden movement caused her to clutch her head and groan.

Chloe sat down on the side of the mattress and put her arm around her daughter. "I'm sorry I had to wake you up like this. I know your head must be killing you. But your daddy and I are going to be leaving in a few minutes."

Anna dropped her hands from her temples and stared anxiously at her mother. "Now? Tonight? Is he—" She was forced to stop and swallow as fear knotted her throat. "Is he injured critically?"

Chloe shook her head. "No...it doesn't sound that serious. The caller said Adam was in the hospital with a broken leg. And that was the only injury he knew about."

"Thank God for that much," Anna murmured as thoughts of her brother whirled through her mind. He'd always been like a third arm or leg to her. Even when they were apart, she always felt his presence, as he did hers. She ached for him now.

"Don't you think I should go, too? I want to see him," she said, quickly throwing back the covers.

"Not tonight," Chloe said quickly. "You don't need to be traveling with that lump on your head. Besides, if it turns out Adam needs surgery on his leg, we might have to stay down there for an extended time. If that's the case, I'll need you here to see after the horses for me."

Anna nodded at her mother's reasoning. "Of course, I'll do anything you need me to."

Chloe hugged her close. "I know you will, darling."

She got up from the bed and gently pushed Anna back down against the pillow. "Try to rest and don't worry. We'll call you as soon as we find out anything. And in the morning please go over to Miguel's and explain to him what's happened and that it looks as though we'll be away for a few days."

"Go over to Miguel's? Mother, there's no need for

that! The man will probably be down at the stables by daybreak. I'll let him know then.''

Chloe frowned at her daughter. ''He won't be down at the stables in the morning. The men are going to be doing roundup without him tomorrow. He was going to Alamogordo to make a deal on some liquid feed.''

''Then I'll tell him when he gets back.''

Chloe shot her an exasperated look. Anna groaned and scrubbed her eyes with both fists. ''I know, Mother. I'm being a pain. It's just that I'm worried sick about Adam, and I'd rather go see him than stay here with…Miguel Chavez! You might as well know right now that we've had…a run-in.''

Chloe made a palms-up gesture as if to tell her daughter so what. ''Then the two of you will just have to get back on track. I can't concentrate on Adam unless I know this place is being taken care of, and that's going to mean both you and Miguel seeing after things.''

Anna always loved having a chance to help her parents, to pay them back for all the wonderful years they'd given her. But why the heck did she have to do it with Miguel Chavez?

''Don't worry,'' Anna assured her mother. ''I won't let you down. If need be, I'll murder Miguel and persuade Lester to come back.''

''Fat chance.'' She headed toward the door, then paused with her hand on the knob. ''By the way, just what did Miguel do to get you so stirred up?''

''Well…'' Anna's mouth opened and closed, then she decided where her mother was concerned honesty was always the best policy. "For starters he...kissed me!"

No stunned gasp or words of outrage. Chloe simply threw back her head and laughed. "I'm sure that was sheer punishment."

Anna flung her tangled red hair out of her eyes. "Humiliating torture."

Chloe chuckled once again. "Oh, Anna, I can see I'm not going to have to worry about you while I'm gone."

Her mother hurried on out the door, and Anna groaned and fell back against the pillows. It was after two o'clock. Morning and dealing with Miguel was going to be here all too soon.

The rambling log house, perched precariously on the side of the mountain, was just as Anna remembered. The front, with its plate-glass windows and wide wooden deck, faced the west and looked out over a deep arroyo. Tall ponderosa pine, spruce and aspen spilled down the rugged bluff behind the house and crowded around the structure, shading the roof and the deck.

Anna had always loved the quiet, rustic beauty of the place. Even though it didn't compare to the splendor of the Bar M hacienda, the house was a lovely one, and the solitude it provided appealed to Anna far more than the bustle of activity that was always going on down at the ranch house.

As she walked across the deck, she wondered if Miguel liked it here in the Hondo Valley, then just as quickly the question of what had brought him to this place floated through her mind.

However, Anna needed to know about Miguel Chavez as much as she needed another kick in the head. So she did her best to thrust the thought from her mind, then squared her shoulders and punched the doorbell.

Long moments passed before the door opened. As Anna stood looking at him across the threshold, she was embarrassed to see she'd caught him in the act of shaving. He was dressed only in a pair of jeans and boots. A small white towel hung around his neck. Anna couldn't help but notice the bold contrast it and the specks of white lather on his face made against his dark skin.

"Sorry about the interruption," she said as coolly as she could manage, "but I needed to talk to you before you left for Alamogordo this morning. And I remembered this place had never had a telephone."

He pulled the towel from his neck and wiped the remaining shaving cream from his jaws and upper lip. "I have a cellular in case of emergencies."

Her mother had failed to tell her that bit of information. The idea Chloe was deliberately throwing her at Miguel deepened the frown that was already marring Anna's face.

"I didn't know," she admitted.

His weight shifted from one boot to the other as though he was waiting for her to continue and was irritated that she hadn't. "Has something happened?" he asked.

She nodded, and he motioned with his head for her to follow him inside. As soon as she passed through the small foyer and into the large living room, Anna was immediately struck by the difference in the place.

All of Lester's and his wife's things were gone, along with the clutter and hominess the older couple lent to the place. The room was now sparsely decorated, yet surprisingly neat and comfortable.

Without waiting for an invitation, she took a seat on a plump sofa covered with brown suede.

"Did you know my twin had gone to South America?" she asked without preamble.

Miguel stood facing her in the middle of the large room, as though sitting would encourage her to stay longer than necessary. Well, he needn't worry, Anna thought. She was going to be out of here like a shot as soon as she got her mother's message over with.

"Yes. Your father had talked to me about his leaving. He hated to see his son go, but he thought it would be good for him and his work."

Anna nodded. "Well, it seems Adam was involved in some sort of accident, and my parents have flown down there to be with him. They left early this morning around two o'clock."

Miguel looked at her sharply. "Was he hurt badly?"

Anna shook her head. "We don't think so. I mean, a broken leg is bad enough, but it doesn't appear to be life threatening."

His expression eased. "Thank God for that."

Anna sighed. "I do."

"So was there something else your mother wanted me to know or do? Does she want me to see after her horses while she's away, or does she want me to hire someone?"

"I'll be taking care of the horses."

Anna rose to her feet, then suddenly wished she

hadn't. She could feel Miguel's dark eyes running up and down the length of her as though he were sizing her up and found her totally lacking.

"You?"

"That's what I said. Do you have a problem with that?"

Other than the faint lift of his brows, his expression didn't alter. "Why don't you go into the kitchen and pour yourself a cup of coffee while I finish dressing."

Why was he going to bother with dressing now? she wondered wildly. She'd already gotten an eyeful, and she hated him for being so blatantly sexy. Now whenever she looked at him, she wouldn't be seeing him in a work shirt. She'd be seeing thick, muscled shoulders and arms, a broad chest and washboard stomach. She wouldn't have to wonder if his face was darker than the rest of him. She would know that beneath his clothes he was a smooth, delicious coffee brown.

Unbidden heat filled her cheeks, and she hoped to heaven he was far enough away to dismiss it for makeup. "Do you have any made?"

He nodded. "But I haven't eaten breakfast yet, have you?"

She shook her head. "I don't want any."

He frowned. "Do you know how to cook or does your mama have to do that for you, too?"

She tried not to show her bristles. "My *mama* doesn't have to do anything for me," she said crisply. "And I know how to cook. Do you?"

He shot her a little mocking smile. "Of course." He turned to leave the room, then tossed over his shoulder, "I'll join you in five minutes."

When Miguel entered the kitchen a short time later, Anna was perched on a bar stool, nursing a mug of coffee. At the sound of his footsteps she turned and looked at him.

Earlier, when he'd discovered her at the front door, Miguel had hardly been able to get his gaze beyond the purplish blue lump on her forehead. But now he was very nearly transfixed at the utterly beautiful picture she made with her bright hair, pale skin and green, green eyes.

She was wearing a rich apricot blouse tucked into a pair of faded jeans. Hand-tooled boots were on her feet and a cream colored felt hat that cost more than an average week's wages hung carelessly from a stampede string against her back. A silver and turquoise cuff bracelet circled her wrist, and tiny turquoise birds dangled from her earlobes.

She epitomized everything he despised in a woman. Yet Miguel was beginning to realize there was more to her than just the surface. And that troubled him. Maybe she wasn't a spoiled little rich girl like Charlene had been. But she was rich and she was young, and he had no business being attracted to her.

"You haven't heard from your parents this morning?"

He went to the refrigerator and pulled out bacon and eggs.

"No. I talked to both my aunts to tell them what happened. Rose and Harlan said to let them know if you need help with anything."

"Rose and Harlan have their own ranch to take care of," he remarked as he slapped several slices of bacon into an iron skillet.

From the corner of her eye Anna watched him work at the gas range. And just as she feared, she wasn't seeing the white cotton shirt he was wearing, she was picturing him without it.

"You don't like Rose and Harlan?" she asked a bit defensively.

"I like them very much. That's why I don't want to overload them with work that you and I can take care of. Or am I being presumptuous in thinking you're going to work out at this job?"

Anna racked her brain trying to recall any man who had infuriated her as much as this one. Yet it was impossible. She'd never met a man like Miguel. Period.

"Don't you mean work, rather than work out?" she asked in a saccharine-sweet voice.

He didn't bother turning to look at her as he tended the sizzling bacon. "However you want to say it, I'm not sure you're up to filling Chloe's boots."

Anna expected he'd made the flip remark to irritate and probably even challenge her. He couldn't know just how insecure, how lacking she felt compared to her mother.

When she failed to reply, Miguel glanced over his shoulder and was surprised to see her staring vacantly into her cup. He'd expected her to be on her feet, blasting away at him.

"What's the matter?"

His voice jerked her back to the moment and she lifted her eyes to him. "Nothing. And don't worry," she added flatly, "I may not be able to win the All American Futurity but I can see the horses are properly taken care of."

"You look like you need to be in bed. That's a hell of a bruise on your forehead. Does it hurt?"

"Aunt Justine came over last night and brought me a few pain pills. Since she's a nurse, she wanted to make sure I didn't have a concussion."

A lesser woman wouldn't have been on her feet today, and that in itself amazed Miguel. "What was your aunt's diagnosis?"

Anna grimaced. "That I have an unusually hard head."

"She wasted a trip. I could have told her that."

Anna couldn't stop herself. There was something about the man that pulled at her. Her mind said she didn't want to be within a hundred yards of him. Yet the rest of her craved to touch him, smell him, kiss his lips all over again.

Sliding from the bar stool, she joined him at the range, yet was careful to keep a few inches between their shoulders. In spite of the pungent smell of the bacon, her nose sniffed out the clean male scent of his skin, the faint musk in his aftershave.

"What are you cooking?" she asked.

"Bacon, eggs and tortillas."

"Don't you know those things aren't good for you?"

His head turned slightly and his eyes settled on her lips. "There's lots of things that aren't good for me."

Heat flared inside Anna like the instant spark of flint against steel, and her heart hummed like a runaway machine. It seemed incredible that only a month ago she thought she would never want another man. But now as she stood close to Miguel, she was fairly certain she was only just now learning what wanting a man was all about. Certainly she'd never felt this raw aching attraction for Scott. Or any man. Until she'd met Miguel. The idea was both exhilarating and frightening.

"Then why do you...indulge yourself?"

He grinned, then looked away from her as he placed tortillas on a hot griddle. Anna was relieved to find she could breathe again.

"A man only has a short time on this earth. To deny himself some of life's basic pleasures is foolish."

Folding her arms against her breast, she watched him fork the crisp bacon onto a paper towel. "So you're not just a cowboy, you're a philosopher, too."

He broke eggs into the bacon grease. "No. Just a cowboy with a few opinions."

The word *few* put a vague smile on Anna's lips. "Is that what you've always been, a cowboy?"

He nodded. "Always a cowboy, and for a time a lawman, too."

Completely surprised by his admission, she stared at him. "Really? What sort of lawman?"

"First as a deputy, then as an undersheriff."

"Around here?"

"No. Bernalillo county."

Her eyes widened. "That would include Albuquerque."

"You're right."

She waited, hoping he would tell her more. But he remained silent as he finished cooking the eggs and warming the tortillas. He worked at the stove with practiced ease, and Anna wondered if he'd learned to cook out of necessity or because he enjoyed it. She got the feeling it was both.

Once the food was done, she helped him carry the dishes to a booth-style table made of varnished knotty pine. The table was built next to a wide-paned window overlooking the backyard. Not that there was an actual backyard. Little more than thirty feet away, the bluff of the mountain rose up like a giant wall of craggy rock, where sage and pine clung tenaciously to the cracks and crevices.

Anna was always mesmerized by the wild beauty surrounding this place, and Miguel must have picked up on the wonder mirrored on her face as she gazed out the window.

"Haven't you ever seen the view behind the house?" he asked as he placed two fresh mugs of coffee beside their plates.

Nodding, Anna took a seat on one side of the table. "Yes. But it's been a long time. My brother and I used to come up here and go hiking and exploring. It's one of my favorite places on the ranch." She looked at him as he took his seat across from her. "My dad first had this built as a honeymoon house for him and Mom. So they'd have a place to go when they wanted to be completely alone. But after a few years it somehow became the foreman's house."

"When I came to work for your mother I had a house just east of Ruidoso," Miguel told her. "I wanted to continue to live there, but Chloe wouldn't hear of it. She wanted me closer for practical purposes and promised that if I sold my house and then later decided I didn't want to work on the Bar M anymore, she'd pay the down payment on another one." He shrugged. "But I fell in love with this place on first sight."

Miguel passed the eggs to Anna, and she began to fill her plate. Her stomach was gnawing and fluttering. Breakfast was what it needed, but she hadn't planned on having it with Miguel. How she'd wound up here at his kitchen table was beyond her. He seemed to have a knack for taking control of her.

"My uncle Roy is the sheriff of Lincoln County," Anna said. "I guess you must know him."

"I've known Roy for many years. He's a legend in his own time."

She shook a goodly amount of Tabasco over her eggs. "Did you not want to make the law your life as Roy has?"

Miguel swallowed several bites of food before he answered. "It was a job. A way to make money. I didn't see it as a career."

"How long did you work as a lawman?"

Anna didn't know if his frown was caused by the effort of calculating or annoyance at being questioned by her. "More than ten years."

His answer was nothing close to what she'd expected and the shock showed on her face. "Ten years! You must have started very young."

One corner of his mouth lifted wryly. "Just how old do you think I am, Anna?"

She felt herself blushing as his dark hazel eyes waited on her face. "I don't know...thirty-five?"

"There was no need for you to be so careful about answering. I don't care if you know I'm thirty-seven."

Thirty seven. He was a decade older than Scott, yet oddly enough, she felt no gap between them. He was simply a man and she a woman, and the hands of time had nothing to do with the breathless way she felt whenever she looked at him or touched him.

"And it really doesn't matter to me whether you know I'm going on twenty-five," she replied. "But I would like to know why you quit being a lawman."

The frown on his face deepened, and he forked a bite of egg from his plate. "Because I like being a cowboy more. Is that answer enough for you?"

The tortilla in her hand stopped midway to her lips. "No," she retorted.

His eyes narrowed and for a moment he completely forgot he was eating breakfast. "Look, Anna, I'm not trying to hide some dark tragedy. I wasn't burned-out or disillusioned. Sure I encountered some hideous sights while I worked in law enforcement, but I was like your uncle Roy. I expected to see the worst and dealt with it as part of the job. It simply comes down to the fact that I'd rather strap on a pair of chaps than a gun every morning. Satisfied?"

As long as she was around this man she would never be satisfied. He was an enigma, a challenge, a man who stirred her far too much.

"Sorry I asked."

"No, you're just sorry you wanted to know," he said with lazy certainty. "You had this grand romantic notion that I have an unbearable festering splinter inside of me and you're the woman to pull it out and make me human and whole again. Well, I don't need healing or consoling or saving."

She stared at him, anger shooting through her like a red-hot arrow. "What in the he—heck am I doing here?"

Before he could answer, she tossed the half-eaten

tortilla onto her plate and jumped to her feet. "I'll be down at the stables. Not that—"

Her words broke off as a wave of dizziness suddenly spun the room around her head. Clutching the edge of the table with one hand, she pressed shaky fingers to the bruise on her forehead.

"Anna! Are you all right?" He got up from the table and put a steadying hand on her arm.

Anna wasn't all right. But not for anything would she admit her weakness to him. "I'm fine. I just got up too quickly. That's all."

He cursed beneath his breath. "You've got a concussion! You shouldn't even be on your feet."

The dizziness finally gone, she dropped her hand and glared at him. "Damn it, I don't have a concussion. And I wish you'd quit acting as though you know everything about me!"

Stung because she'd mocked his concern, he sneered at her. "If you don't have a concussion, what's wrong with you? Are you pregnant? Is that why you suddenly decided to come home to your mama and daddy?"

Stunned by his impertinent questions, her mouth fell open. "Are you crazy? Do you think I would have been working in the branding pen out in the heat if I were in such a condition?"

His jaw tightened and his eyes darkened. "I've known women to do worse."

"Well, not me!" she gritted in outrage. "Besides, you know I'm not married."

His brows lifted mockingly. "A person doesn't have to be married to have children. Or haven't you learned that yet?"

He was just the sort of man to point such a thing out, Anna thought angrily. "You have to be the most insolent...most arrogant—"

"Sit down and finish your breakfast," he ordered.

"It's finished! And so are we," she said defiantly.

Suddenly his fist was full of her red hair, and he used it to tug her up against him. With a cruel chuckle, he said, "There is no 'we.' Or is that what you're really wanting, Anna? Is this what you're pushing me to do?"

He didn't give her a chance to answer. His head bent at the same time he jerked on her hair, forcing her face up to his.

"Yes," he whispered huskily, his narrowed eyes roaming her flushed face. "I think this is what you really want."

"Miguel—"

His name was the only word he allowed her to speak. The rest he smothered with the brazen search of his lips. And all Anna could do was cling to the front of his shirt and try not to wilt at his feet.

"You kiss me like I'm the only man you've ever wanted," he murmured.

He was making fun of her, but his words were so close to the truth she shuddered inwardly.

"You're not the only man I've ever kissed!" she tried to defend herself, but her voice was weak and trembling.

He looked at her with hard, hooded eyes. "I didn't say I was the only man you'd kissed. I said the only man you had wanted. There's a big difference, Anna. And I'm warning you not to try and spread your virgin wings on me."

"As if I'd want to! And my being a virgin is hardly your business!"

Ignoring her sarcasm, he said, "You and I are two different breeds, Anna. I know what you are, and I know what I am. We won't go together like tortillas and honey."

How could he know about her? Anna wondered. And why did she want him to know the real woman she was, not the one he believed her to be? He was overbearing and impudent. But most of all he was a man. And she'd sworn never to want another one!

Jerking her arm from his grasp, she stepped around him. "I'm very relieved to hear that, Miguel. So you take care of your end of things on the ranch, and I'll take care of mine. Savvy?"

"Completely."

Not bothering to give him a backward glance, Anna left the room. She was across the deck and on the way down the steps to her truck when Miguel's deep voice called after her.

Glancing over her shoulder, she tried to steel herself against the sight of his hard, handsome image outlined by the mountain bluff behind him. He fit this land like a hand to a glove. But then so did she. He just didn't know it.

"I'm going to be watching you."

Turning to face him, she pushed back the brim of her hat and stared up at him. "Excuse me. I thought you were the foreman around here, not the lord of the manor."

"I can be both. If need be."

In other words if she couldn't take care of the place

while her parents were gone, he certainly could. And would, if she so much as faltered a step.

Well, she wouldn't stumble or stagger, she silently averred. And Mr. Miguel Chavez was going to have to eat every hateful word he'd ever said to her before she left the Bar M.

Chapter Four

Anna replaced the phone on its cradle, then fell back against the cushions of the couch in a dazed thump. Adam was going to be fine. His broken ankle had already been set and put in a plaster cast. Tomorrow he would be released from the hospital. The news was exactly what she'd been desperately wanting to hear all morning. It was the rest of her mother's message that had knocked Anna's feet out from under her.

What had been her parents' thinking? Or more rightly her mother? Of course Anna could see it was a perfect time for the two of them to travel on down to the coast of Brazil and enjoy a second honeymoon. But Anna had been away from the ranch for more than a year! And even longer still since she'd done any real work around the place. Did her parents actually think she was capable of seeing after the horses for three weeks or a month?

It wasn't that Anna was afraid of manual labor. In

fact, she welcomed the release it gave her after hours of sitting at the piano day after day. But the responsibility of seeing after two barns full of highbred racehorses was something else altogether. What if one became injured or ill? What if she exercised them too much or too little? They'd all be so stiff and sore they'd never be able to run to a feed bucket, much less down a race track.

And then there was Miguel. The man was insufferable. He'd be watching her every move. No doubt he'd take great pleasure in seeing her fall on her face.

Rising from the couch, she wandered restlessly over to the piano. The lid was down and had been that way since she'd arrived home four days ago. So far she'd had no desire to make any sort of music.

Her fingers trailed absently over the wood as thoughts of this morning burned once again in her mind. Miguel believed she wasn't capable of doing anything except play the piano. And no doubt he'd roar a loud complaint when he heard Chloe had left her in charge for the next month. But Anna wasn't one dimensional. There was more to her than making music and pleasing an audience. Moreover, her parents had put their faith and trust in her. If need be she'd work twenty-four hours a day to make sure things ran smoothly. And in the process she'd show Miguel Chavez that she was not just a coddled performer who knew nothing of the real world!

When Miguel rode in from roundup later that evening, darkness had overtaken the ranch yard. All of the cowhands had chosen to stay with the chuck wagon and bed down in sleeping bags rather than ride back to the ranch. But Miguel had felt the need to come back to the Bar M. With her parents gone, he didn't want Anna to be entirely alone.

She might think she was perfectly capable of handling things around here. But Miguel knew better. Three days from now she'd be crying for him to take over.

A glance at his watch told him it was nearly nine. A late hour for him to be out on a horse, but he seriously doubted Anna would be in bed. As soon as he unsaddled and tended to his mount, he'd walk down to the house and speak with her. Hopefully she had news of Adam.

The many working horses on the Bar M were stalled in a separate barn, several yards away from Chloe's high-strung racing stock. As he led the tired animal past the stables of Thoroughbreds, he noticed a shaft of light beneath the closed doors. Figuring Anna had forgotten to turn it off, he made a mental note to stop and check it before he left the ranch yard.

Twenty minutes later, on his way back by the stables, he noticed the light was still burning. He opened the doors to extinguish it and was instantly shocked to see Anna at the opposite end of the building. One hand held a galvanized pail, while the other gripped a thick lead rope attached to a skittish yearling, who followed closely on her shoulder.

Miguel walked quickly down the alleyway to intercept her. Once he was within a few steps, she stopped and lifted her head to look at him. For a moment all Miguel could do was stare back, stunned at her appearance. Gone were the expensive clothes, hat and boots. They had been replaced by worn jeans and shirt, work boots and a baseball cap. Yet the clothes were only a part of the drastic change. The woman was bone-weary exhausted. He could see it in the dark smudges beneath her eyes and the deep lines bracketing her mouth. The bruise on her temple looked even more purple against her white face.

"Anna, what are you doing?"

She gave him a look that said his question had to be the most ignorant she'd ever heard. "I'm taking care of the horses. What does it look like?"

He made a point of glancing at his wristwatch. "At this time of night? Your mother never works this late. Not even on a race day."

Anna wanted to snap at him, to remind him that she wasn't her mother. But she wouldn't give him the satisfaction of knowing she was riled or rattled. She knew how to be cool and by damn she would be.

Squaring her shoulders as best she could, she said, "Maybe it slipped your mind that all the hands are out on roundup. It takes time for one person to feed and water thirty head of horses."

Miguel felt like kicking himself. He'd been so busy he'd not thought to send a couple of the men back to help her. Anna must surely be thinking he'd purposely kept every ranch hand for his own needs.

"I guess I owe you an apology."

Anna didn't want his apologies, she wanted his respect. But it looked as though she was going to have to earn that the hard way. "Forget it. I'd rather care for the horses myself than trust a cowboy to do it right."

She led the horse on past him, and Miguel automatically followed. Every masculine cell inside him wanted to take the pail of water from her hand and carry it for her. But from her remark he could only believe she would resent his help.

Angry at himself, and at her, but not really sure why, he blurted out, "You shouldn't be out here working this late." Hell, she shouldn't have been here at all, Miguel thought. Not with that goose egg on her forehead.

"I'm fine."

Deciding it would be best to let it go at those two words, Miguel watched her lead the young horse into a stall and unsnap the lead rope from the colt's halter. "Have you heard from your parents yet? How is your brother?"

The concern in his voice caused Anna to glance at him. "My brother is going to be fine. They've placed his foot in a cast and he'll be released from the hospital tomorrow."

Anna couldn't help but notice Miguel was visibly relieved. The fact that he was concerned for her brother touched her. Adam was so much a part of her. Even when they were apart, which had been often these past few years, she always felt his presence with her.

"So when are Chloe and Wyatt coming home? Tomorrow?"

Anna filled the yearling's water bucket, then stepped out of the stall. "No. They won't be heading back for a while."

He pushed the brim of his dirty felt hat back off his forehead. "What's happened? Adam needs them down there?"

She let out a laugh that had nothing to do with humor. "Independent Adam? Not hardly. He's determined to finish the job down there on crutches, so my parents have suddenly decided now would be a good time for them to travel on down to the coast and spend the next few weeks on a second honeymoon."

Miguel looked incredulous. "You're not serious, are you?"

Anna wearily pushed a tangle of red curls off her forehead and leaned her shoulder against the stall door. "This is hardly a time to be joking."

"But why would they do something like that now? You're here on vacation. Looks to me as though they'd want to spend some time with you."

"There will be plenty of time for them to be with me once they get back. I'm sure you've seen for yourself that Mother rarely ever takes a vacation away from the ranch. And Daddy will thoroughly love having her all to himself."

Miguel's expression of dismay didn't alter. "Both your parents work very hard. I understand all that. But to leave you with all this to care for." He gestured at the row of stalled horses and shook his head. "I'm going to be honest with you, this is very much out of character for them."

Not for anything would Anna let him know she'd been thinking the very same thing. She'd taken heart in the fact that her parents didn't doubt her capabilities of caring for the ranch. But was she really? Could she get through the next few weeks without making a fool of herself and a mess of everything? Were her parents trying to test her for some reason?

"I suppose they were thinking it's a rare day when one of their children is available to take over for them.

I'm here, and they asked me if I would handle seeing after the ranch. I was hardly going to disappoint them by saying no."

"Well that's just dandy," he muttered. "They leave you here with a concussion and a lump on your forehead as big as a golf ball and expect you to take care of things."

Frowning, Anna's fingers lifted to her forehead. "I don't have a concussion, and there's hardly a lump there at all now."

Miguel snorted. "You look like you're ready to fall over."

Before she realized what he was about to do, he snatched up both her hands and studied her palms. The soft skin just below her fingers was broken and bleeding. Not wanting him to see the damage, she tried to jerk them loose from his grip, but he tightened his hold.

"I knew Chloe was wrong about you. Any normal cowgirl would know to wear a pair of work gloves. Now you've got a pair of ruined hands to go with a concussion!"

Anna tried to glare at him, but the touch of his hands so firmly wrapped around hers was sending her senses in all sorts of wild directions. The most she could do was stare at him in bewilderment.

"For the last time—I don't have a concussion. And for your information, I've had on a pair of gloves all day. I only took them off a few minutes ago."

"Just as I figured. You're so soft even a pair of gloves don't help."

"What do you know about it?" Anna muttered, hating the smugness in his voice.

''I know you look ready to fall in your tracks at any moment.''

Her gaze made a slow, deliberate sweep of his tall muscular body. Dirt, manure and grass stained the entire front of his jeans and a good measure of his denim shirt. Dust coated the faint stubble of beard on his chin and jaws. His eyes were bloodshot from long hours in the sun. And in that one long glance, Anna felt herself melting like a cube of sugar in a cup of hot coffee. He was a man who worked hard for himself and for her parents. She greatly respected him for that.

''You don't exactly look ready for the hundred-yard dash yourself,'' she replied.

''I'm used to this. You're not.''

Anna was dead on her feet, but as she'd discovered beforehand there was something about Miguel that made her want to linger in his presence, to find out the mysteries behind his dark hazel eyes.

Shaking her hair back over her shoulders, she leveled her gaze on his face and sighed with irritation. ''I suppose you think my job doesn't require long hours.''

''I'm sure I don't know what it requires. But I do know you don't come away from the piano like this.'' His lips thinned to a line of disgust as he looked once again at torn flesh on her palms. ''Come on. Let's go down to the house and I'll fix them for you.''

Beneath the brim of the baseball cap, Anna's brows arched with dismay. ''Fix them? I have a few blisters, Miguel. I don't need stitches!''

Miguel would like to tell her exactly what he thought she needed, but he was too exhausted to have a round with her tonight. Besides, he seriously doubted she'd be able to make it out of bed in the morning. And once that happened he'd be in the clear to hire someone to take care of the horses.

"These hands need to be cleaned and dressed, just the same."

"I can't take a shower with bandages on my hands. And I can hardly go to bed like this!" She looked pointedly down at the front of her dirty clothes.

"I'll wait for you to get out of the shower." He dropped her hands, but before Anna could breathe a sigh of relief that he was no longer touching her, he took her by the shoulder and urged her out of the stables.

"Maybe Chloe will have some leftovers in the fridge," he said. "I rode out of camp before Cook had supper ready."

"You raid my parents refrigerator often?" she asked drily.

He switched off the lights and the two of them stepped outside. As he turned to fasten the double doors, he said, "Whenever I can catch them gone. I steal their jewels and sell them for whiskey money, too."

"You're so funny."

He glanced at her shadowed face. The only smile he'd seen on her face had been a mocking one. He was beginning to doubt the woman knew how to really smile. "I can assure you, you're not a bit amusing."

She made a disgusted sound in her throat. "I didn't realize I was supposed to be making you laugh."

"What about making yourself laugh?"

His question took her by surprise. But before she could think of any sort of response, he took her by the elbow and headed them both down the trodden path to the house.

Once inside, Anna left him to his own company and hurried away to the shower. Miguel washed his hands in the kitchen sink and made a quick search of the refrigerator. Just as he expected, there was half a casserole of beef enchiladas. He put them in the microwave to heat and went about making a tossed salad.

By the time Anna reappeared, he had the table set for two and strong coffee brewing. The wide-toothed comb she'd been dragging through her wet hair stopped in midair as her gaze went from him to the waiting supper.

"You weren't kidding about getting into the refrigerator," she said.

A wan smile touched his lips. "No. Your parents have always encouraged me to make myself at home here. And I do at times, when it's more convenient than going up to the honeymoon house."

So he felt comfortable here in the ranch house. Somehow she resented that. In a little more than a year he was certain about belonging to this place. Anna had grown up here on the ranch and in this very house, yet she wasn't at all sure she belonged here anymore. She wanted to, but so many things had changed while she'd been away. Or was it she who had changed?

Miguel gestured toward the table. "If you want to take a seat, I'll see to your hands before we eat."

Anna wanted to tell him he had a thing about authority and taking control, but she kept the opinion to herself. In his own way the man was trying to help her, and she didn't want to appear ungrateful.

Slipping her comb into the pocket of her robe, she

took a seat at the empty end of the table and laid her palms upward on the tabletop. Miguel fetched a first aid kit from a cabinet over the refrigerator. Then taking a seat across from her, picked several items from the plastic case.

As he poured peroxide over the wounds, Miguel wanted to curse at the sight of her marred skin, but he forced himself to bite back the choice words on his lips. The damage was already done. And for the next month he was going to have to try to get along with this woman.

"Have you always been a stubborn girl?" he asked as he dabbed at the broken skin with a cotton ball.

Trying not to wince, Anna said, "Not really. My brother Adam is the stubborn one. When he gets a notion in his head, there's no changing it."

"Humph. If you two didn't look so much alike I would doubt you were twins. You're nothing like your brother."

"In what way?" she asked, curious that he'd made any sort of assumption about her, other than that she was a pampered rose.

He lifted his head and looked at her. Anna once again felt undressed as his dark gaze drifted to where her blue silk robe parted at the vee between her breasts.

"Your brother appears to be an uncomplicated guy."

She desperately needed to gulp in a long breath of air, but she forced herself to breathe as slowly as possible, to behave as though his gaze, his touch, did not affect her at all.

"If that's what you think, then you don't know Adam. He's had his own demons to deal with."

His lips twisted. "Everybody has those. At least he's kept a sense of humor about him. He can and does laugh."

"I haven't exactly seen you splitting your sides since I met you," she remarked coolly.

He unfastened the cap on a tube of ointment and gently smeared it over the ragged skin. "Most people aren't up to laughing when they've had a splitting, clawing tigress thrown at them."

Pain from her hands and anger at him had Anna gritting her teeth. "You really are insufferable. It's no wonder you live alone up there in the honeymoon house."

Miguel's gaze shifted to her face. As he made a lazy search of her features, Anna felt her heart begin to beat faster and faster. She'd never met a man so commanding, so totally and utterly male.

"I live alone because I choose to. Not because I have to."

His attention turned back to his task, and for long moments Anna contented herself to study the wave in his thick dark hair, the way his big hands moved so nimbly. He smelled of sweat and dust, cattle and horses and sage. The combined scents were exotic, lusty, a strong aphrodisiac to her senses.

"Mother said you were married once," she said before she could stop the words.

He didn't look up. "She was right," he said bluntly. "I was married. Once."

"I don't suppose you'd want to tell me what happened?"

He glanced up long enough for her to see the frown on his face. "What do you mean, what happened?"

She shrugged. "I mean why you aren't still married."

He reached for a piece of gauze and gently placed it across the affected area of her hand. "I guess you could say she wanted more than I could give her."

He sounded bitter, and Anna wondered how long it had been since he'd gotten divorced. From the impression her mother had given her, a long time. If that was the case, his lingering sourness meant he'd either loved his wife very much or hated the very sight of her. She longed to know which, though she couldn't understand why.

Miguel ripped off several strips of adhesive tape and fastened the pads of gauze to both her hands. Once he was satisfied the bandages would stay in place, he put all the first aid items back into their small case, then left the table to put it away.

Anna tentatively flexed her fingers and was relieved to find the stinging soreness wasn't nearly as bad as it had been earlier. "This does feel much better, Miguel. Thank you."

Her appreciation for his nursing took him off guard. He'd grown so used to Anna's cutting remarks he hadn't been expecting any sort of thanks. And he suddenly realized this woman was everything but predictable.

"You're welcome," he murmured, then feeling more awkward than he could ever remember, he turned his attention to putting the food on the table.

They had both filled their plates and taken several

bites before the silence in the room was broken by Anna.

"I don't think you told me why you came back to the ranch tonight. Wouldn't it have been easier to have stayed at the roundup camp with the other men? Now you'll have that long ride back in the morning."

He glanced up from the steaming enchilada on his plate, then quickly wished he hadn't. The sight of Anna with her wet curls and flimsy robe was enough to turn any man's thoughts. Yet it was not her sexiness that was touching the deepest part of him. It was her frail, battered appearance. The purple bruise against her white face. Her bandaged hands trying to maneuver the simple act of eating. She was so young and innocent in many ways. And yet there was a weariness in her eyes that said she'd lived far too much too fast.

"I wanted to see if you'd heard news from Adam. And I...well, I wasn't too keen about leaving the ranch so deserted."

"I'm here. The place wouldn't have been totally empty. Besides, no one ever makes mischief on the Bar M. I don't suppose anything bad has happened on this place since—" She broke off and her mouth parted as she realized what she'd been about to say.

He studied her for a few moments, then said, "Since Belinda Waller tried to burn it down twenty odd years ago."

Her brows lifted with even more surprise. "You know the story?"

He hesitated, then nodded. "I wasn't sure if you did. I shouldn't have said anything."

She met his gaze head-on as though to assure him she wasn't ashamed of how she and her twin came to be born. "Adam and I have known for years that Belinda Waller was our birth mother and Tomas Murdock was our actual father. Chloe and Wyatt never tried to keep the truth a secret from us or anyone. In fact, our parents always encouraged us to be proud of our heritage. And we are proud. At least I'm fairly certain Adam is. And I am, too."

His expression solemn, he studied her face. "I hear a *but* in there somewhere."

Anna found she couldn't look at him, and she wasn't at all sure why. She wasn't ashamed of her mother. She simply had mixed emotions about her.

"I guess it's hard for me to accept that she left me and my brother on the porch of this ranch as if we were no more than a basket of laundry."

He let out a sigh. He didn't want to feel anything for this woman. She was far richer than most women could ever dream of being. Yet he could see shadows of pain behind her pale green eyes, and that bothered Miguel. He of all people knew what it was like to hurt, to be betrayed by the one you loved.

"From what I understand she was a troubled woman on drugs at the time. She thought she was leaving you in the care of your father."

"Yes. She didn't know he was already dead from a heart attack. Realistically I understand all that. I guess it's the maternal instinct in me that cringes at the idea of giving up your own flesh and blood. And then to think she tried to burn the ranch down and nearly killed my Aunt Rose and Uncle Harlan in the process. It's not something I want to go around repeating to just anyone. I'm surprised you knew about her."

"I imagine the story of Belinda and Tomas will always be repeated by the people in Lincoln County. Especially with you twins being a reminder of their affair."

Earlier, Anna's stomach had been craving food, now she wasn't sure if she could finish what was left on her plate. She forced herself to swallow several bites, then said, "Belinda kept a journal of that time in her life. Daddy has kept it all these years. When Adam and I were teenagers he let us read it in hopes that we might understand her better. But I'm not sure if I'll ever understand what motivated her to do the things she did. I like to think it was love."

Miguel hadn't expected her to speak of her family so candidly to him. Up until now, she'd seemed to resent the least little question he'd put to her. The fact that she'd opened herself up to him both pleased and bothered Miguel. He didn't want to be tugged, willingly or not, toward this woman. Yet he could feel something inside of him going out to her, and he was helpless to stop it.

"I can't speak for her, but I do know your parents love all of you children very much."

The corners of her lips tilted upward. "We couldn't have better parents than Chloe and Wyatt," she agreed, then cast him a curious glance. "What about you, Miguel? Have you never had family in this area?"

He shook his head. "My father died several years ago of a stroke. After that my mother went back to Mexico to live with her sister."

"Were your parents originally from Mexico?"

"My father was a U.S. citizen. My mother was from

the old country. I think that's one reason why she went back. She feels more at home there.''

"Do you have siblings?"

"A younger sister. She lives in Colorado. I don't get to see her nearly enough."

His remark surprised Anna. He didn't seem like a family man at all. To Anna he was more like a lone wolf, who needed no one but himself. But first impressions could be wrong, and who knew what she might learn about him before her time here on the ranch came to a close.

Across the table from her, Miguel finished the last few bites from his plate, then left the table to fetch the coffeepot. When he started to refill Anna's cup she placed her hand over the rim.

"No, thanks. I couldn't eat or drink another bite. Besides, I don't want the caffeine to keep me awake."

"You should be tired enough to sleep in spite of it," he told her.

As Anna watched him carry the pot back over to its warming plate, she thought of the many nights this past year she'd suffered insomnia. Working herself to the point of exhaustion had never seemed to help. As soon as her head hit the pillow, all sorts of questions, doubts and worries would plague her like an unshakable fever.

And in the end her troubled thoughts would always travel back to the Bar M and her family. Anna had never realized just how much she'd missed both until four days ago when she'd rounded the bend in the lane and had seen the white hacienda and its red tiled roof sparkling in the bright New Mexican sunlight.

Restless and edgy now that the simple meal was

coming to a close, Anna pushed herself to her feet and carried her plate over to the sink. Her legs felt ridiculously weak, and she leaned heavily against the counter. Not for anything did she want Miguel to know just how physically taxing the day had been to her.

"Anna?"

Was that his voice right behind her ear? She started to turn and look and then she felt his breath ruffling her hair and his fingers curve around her upper arm.

"I don't want to seem inhospitable, Miguel," she said quietly. "But I think I'd better say good-night and go to bed."

His sigh was full of relief. "For once we are in agreement," he said, then before Anna could guess his intentions, one arm came around her shoulders, the other beneath the backs of her knees.

She gasped as he lifted her up and into his arms. "Miguel! What—are you doing?"

"Where is your bed?"

His body was warm, his eyes dark and hooded. As Anna's gaze met his she felt what little strength she had left draining away. Even if she'd wanted to she couldn't have fought him. But oddly enough she didn't want to resist him. The iron strength of his arms was like a haven, a place she never wanted to leave.

"Why?" she asked huskily.

"Because I'm going to carry you there," he murmured. "And don't tell me you don't need me. I'm not in any mood to hear it."

Oh, Anna needed him all right. But not in the way he believed. She needed him to hold her, love her, reaffirm to her that she was a wanted woman.

But Miguel *didn't* want her. Not in the same way she was wanting him. He simply felt beholden to take care of her because of her parents.

Oh, dear God, she prayed as he carried her through the living room and down the hallway to the bedrooms. What was she going to do now?

In the darkened hall, she pointed out the door to her room. Miguel carried her through it, then across the plush carpet to a queen-size bed. After laying her gently atop the quilted blue coverlet, he straightened and looked down at her.

"I really think I should stay here tonight, Anna."

She stared at him with wide eyes, while inside the word *no* clawed to get past her throat. But to her horror she swallowed the protest down, then slowly nodded.

Chapter Five

The alarm clock buzzed like a pesky fly in Anna's ear. She swatted at it, missed the button and knocked the whole thing to the floor. Thankfully the noise ceased and she dared to open her eyes.

The room was still pitch-black. What time had she set that darn alarm for, anyway? Leaning up on one elbow, she peeked at the glowing numerals and instantly let out a loud groan. Every muscle in her body felt as though it had been stretched to the limit, then beaten with a club. And her hands! They were both so stiff it was impossible to close her fingers against her palms.

The bandages brought Miguel instantly to her mind and with him a sweep of heat through her entire body. She could only thank God he hadn't been able to read her thoughts last night. Otherwise she didn't think she could ever face the man again. As it was, he'd not guessed the flare of attraction she'd felt for him last night when he'd carried her to bed.

When he'd told her good-night and that he'd be in the guest bedroom if she should need him, she'd felt such a knife of disappointment she didn't know how she'd kept it from her face. And then embarrassment had settled in.

How could she have thought, even for a moment, that he would consider making love to her? The man didn't even like her!

Closing her eyes, she groaned again. Her body and her pride might be bruised, she told herself, but she couldn't continue to lie in bed and wallow in self-pity. She had to get up and get going. The horses would be hungry and pawing to be let loose from their stalls.

As another thought struck her, she glanced toward the closed door of her bedroom. She'd slept so soundly last night, she didn't know if Miguel had actually stayed here in the ranch house as he'd promised. He might have decided she could fend for herself and gone on up the mountain to sleep in his own bed.

Tossing back the covers, she hurriedly reached for her robe. Five minutes later she entered the kitchen, expecting to find Miguel already cooking breakfast and accusing her of being lazy. But the room was empty.

The smell of coffee still lingered in the air, and she walked over to the pot on the counter. She was reaching for a clean cup when, from the corner of her eye, she spotted a small note pinned to the refrigerator.

Forgetting the coffee for a moment, Anna slipped the square of paper from under a magnet of bananas and read: "Anna, I've headed back to the roundup. As soon as I get there I'll send back a couple of men to help you. Miguel."

Anna flipped the paper over, but there was nothing written on the other side. Not that she expected more than what he'd said. But he could have at least mentioned when he would be back.

You don't need to know when the man will be back. He wasn't her boss, Anna firmly reminded herself. She didn't need him to tell her how to take care of a barnful of horses. From the time she'd been old enough to walk, she'd been on or around the animals. Throughout her growing-up years, Anna had wanted only to stay on the Bar M and help her mother train and race.

But her parents and everyone else had told her how brilliant she was at the piano. And how it would be such a shame to waste all that talent. And raising and training horses was a physically demanding job. Playing the piano was a much more refined profession.

The memory of those early years put a grimace on Anna's face as she poured herself a mug of coffee and carried it over to the kitchen table. Refinement had never been her cup of tea, but she'd made herself give up her tomboyish pleasures. She'd tried to convince herself she was a lady of the arts, not a cowgirl. She'd put aside her own desires and done what was expected of her. And now here she was years later with a chance to fulfill her lost dream. Even if it was for only a month's time.

The mug in Anna's hand stopped halfway to her lips. Was that what her mother and father were actually doing? she wondered. Giving her the chance to see what she had in her piano career and what she'd missed here on the ranch?

She'd told her mother she was going to use her time here on the Bar M to try and figure out what she wanted to do with her life. Well, she would. And maybe she would find out that music was her one and only calling. But first she had a foreman to deal with. And she was going to gain his respect even if it killed her!

The cool evening wind rushed past Anna's face and whipped her red hair into a flag behind her as she urged the chestnut Thoroughbred around the circle of dirt track.

She could feel the joy of running in the animal beneath her and Anna absorbed his pleasure. She gave him the bit of rein he was begging for, then laughed with pure delight as his lope became an all-out gallop. With her seat off the saddle and her head against his neck, she urged him to give her everything around the half-mile track.

Anna didn't notice the man on the hill until she'd pulled the horse up and stood tall in the stirrups. As the horse snorted and danced with the urge to keep running, she sawed on the reins and watched Miguel stride off the hill as if a thunderstorm was right behind his shoulder.

Anna forced the horse to walk rather than run around the track one more time, then pulled him to a halt where Miguel stood waiting for her.

"I see you made it in earlier tonight," she said. "How did things go out at roundup?"

"Things went fine at roundup. I came in early to check on you, and looks like it's a damn good thing I did. What are you trying to do? Kill yourself?"

From the look on his face, Anna got the impression he was itching to reach up and drag her off the Thoroughbred. And for one hysterical moment, she wondered what was keeping him from doing it. He wasn't a bashful man. Nothing he could do would surprise her.

"I'm not suicidal," she told him coolly. Then, jumping to the ground, she began to lead the hot horse up the hill toward the stables.

Miguel cursed beneath his breath as he was forced to follow. "It sure as hell looked like it to me. What were you doing on this horse? This is one of Chloe's best runners."

"I know. Isn't he wonderful?"

He looked over at her and was bewildered to see a smile on her face. Not just a hint of one, but an all-out full-of-pleasure smile. And to think a damned horse had put it there. He would never understand this woman.

"Wonderful!" he growled. "If you'd fallen off at the speed you were going it would have snapped your neck like a dry twig!"

She laughed, and if anything, Miguel's expression grew even darker.

"I haven't fallen off a horse since I was six years old," she assured him. "And that only happened because Adam was being pesky and stuck a hotshot to my pony's rump to make him buck."

"Well, this animal—" he gestured to the steaming, snorting horse between them, "is not a pony. And furthermore, I don't ever want to see you on another racehorse again!"

Anna's mouth flew open, then clamped shut. She stalked on up the hill and attached the horse to a mechanical walker. Once he was moving at a cool-down

pace, she headed over to Miguel who had stopped and
waited for her at the open door of the stables.

With the bridle slung over her shoulder, bits of alfalfa clinging to her long braid, and horse hair and
sweat staining the inner legs of her worn jeans, she
looked as though she belonged here on the Bar M, as
if this was the life she was meant for. But Miguel
knew there was another side to her. And this image
he was seeing now was only a momentary break from
her real world.

"I think," she began in a cold, gritty voice, "you'd
better understand right now that you don't give me
orders. Of any kind."

Miguel's jaws clamped with anger. "Do you think
I'm going to stand around and let you jeopardize your
own safety and that of Chloe's horses, just because
you get the whim to play jockey? If you do think that,
then you're far more foolish than I ever imagined!"

Anna had thought she'd felt fury before. The rage
rising up in her was thick, black and choking. It was
all she could do to keep from striking him. But her
long years of hiding her true emotions were enough
to keep her fists clenched at her sides.

"Apparently you've slept too hard, Mr. Chavez, or
you would remember that Chloe left me in charge of
the horses."

"I'm aware of that," he snapped. "But she didn't
mean to give you a free rein! Literally!"

Anna's chin lifted with challenge. "And who did
you think was going to do the galloping? Those two
cowboys you sent back to the ranch to help me?" She
laughed as though the idea was the height of absurdity.
"They both weigh close to two hundred pounds, and

neither of them have ever been on a racehorse. Nor do either of them want to be. They were so scared of being kicked or pawed, I was barely able to talk them into giving the animals a bath!''

"I'll deal with the two men. As for the galloping, you could hire some boy from The Downs in Ruidoso to do it for you.''

"But there's no need for that when I'm here. My mother entrusted me to do it. And I'll not disappoint her.''

Miguel's angry expression turned to one of shocked disbelief. "Your mother knows you were going to gallop? I don't believe it!''

Anna's nostrils flared as she tried to control her temper. "She gave me careful instructions over the phone for each horse. So now that we've got that settled, maybe you'll let me finish my work.''

As Anna started to step past him, Miguel reached out and snagged her by the forearm. She pinned a hard glare on his face, then deliberately dropped her gaze to his brown fingers clamped into her soft skin.

"I don't believe you! Chloe wouldn't want you risking your neck—''

Her eyes flew back to his. "Do you think my mother risks her neck when she gallops?''

"No. Your mother has ridden for years. She knows all about high-strung Thoroughbreds. Whereas you—''

"Only know how to play the piano for an audience,'' she finished for him. A mocking smile tilted the corners of her lips. "Well, there's a lot more to me than what you think you see.''

Her icy confidence goaded Miguel as nothing else

had. He tugged on her arm, and she lurched forward. Before she could regain her balance, his thumb and forefinger clamped around her chin and forced her body to lean into his.

"And there's far more to me than you'll ever know, Miss Anna Sanders," he muttered roughly. "So don't push me! I am the foreman on this ranch. Not you! I am the one who will have to answer to your parents if you wind up in the hospital with a broken neck!"

Her gaze rapidly scanned his green-brown eyes, the angry, mocking lines bracketing his lips. Last night when he'd gently doctored her hands, she'd actually believed he was a compassionate man. What a misjudgment that had been!

"I should have known it was your own neck you were concerned about. Not mine."

"Damn right," he muttered. "I learned a long time ago how you high-society girls work. The only thing you're concerned about is your own personal pleasure and to hell with anyone else!"

In spite of her efforts to stop it, angry color flooded her cheeks. "You have no right or reason to speak to me this way!"

Miguel's eyes dropped to her lips, and suddenly he was lost as to what they were saying, even to where they were. "I have no right or reason to do this, either," he said, his voice dropping to a coarse whisper.

He tugged on her chin so the last few inches between their faces disappeared, then he captured the softness of her lips beneath his.

Incensed that he should want to kiss her after all the insulting things he'd said, Anna squirmed and groaned in protest, but his grip on her chin was like an iron claw. She brought her hands against his chest and shoved, then whimpered as pain shot through her sore palms.

The sound eventually penetrated Miguel's lost senses. Slowly he eased his lips away from hers, then, with his hold still on her jaw, he studied her flushed face.

"I don't know what it is you do to me, Anna. But whatever it is has to be bad."

In spite of all he'd said and his wish to punish her, Anna could not resist the touch of his hand on her face, the strong circle of his arm around her shoulders. Bitter words had spilled from his lips, yet she had never tasted anything so sweet, so all consuming. It made no sense. No sense at all.

"Why is it bad?" she whispered, as her earlier anger was swiftly replaced with bewilderment. "Because you don't like being human?"

"No. Because I don't like being reminded—"

He broke off suddenly, and Anna felt a great disappointment as a shutter fell over his face. Like him, she did not understand why she wanted to slap him one moment, then make love to him the next. But she wanted to understand. She wanted to know what was really behind his dark, handsome face, his shadowed eyes.

"Of her?" Anna ventured quietly.

He looked at her blankly for a few moments, and then his head shook slowly back and forth as he realized she meant his ex-wife. "No. Not of her. Of my own foolishness."

As soon as his words were out, he released her as abruptly as he'd taken hold of her. Anna stared, stunned, as he turned and headed into the dim, cool stables.

"Miguel?"

At the sound of his name, he paused, then glanced over his shoulder at her.

"I'm sorry that you don't want me to gallop the horses. I'm sorry that you don't want me here on the ranch. But I'm going to do what I have to do. And you're going to have to trust me."

Trust her. Maybe in time, where the horses and the ranch were concerned, he would be able to put his faith in her. But one thing he was certain of—he could never entrust her with his heart.

"We'll see, Anna."

He walked away from her then, and it was all Anna could do not to run after him, to provoke him into taking her into his arms one more time. But of course she couldn't. She would be crazy to. She had to go on as she always did and hide the wishes in her heart.

A sadness such as she'd never felt settled over her, and as she walked back out to the chestnut, tears glazed her eyes, then spilled onto her cheeks.

"I don't care if you have to bite their ears or put a damn twitch on their noses! If Miss Sanders tells you to do something to any of those horses, you do it! I don't want her coming back and reporting to me that you two were too afraid to do your job!"

"But, Mr. Chavez," one of the young cowhands spoke up, "we hired on here as cowboys. We don't know nothin' about racing stock."

Miguel's dark eyes grew to dangerous slits. "I've got cowboys running out my ears around here. I need two grooms. If you're too damn ignorant to learn what Miss Sanders shows you to do, then hit the road! I'll find somebody that can.''

The two young cowboys shuffled their feet, mumbled they'd do their best and headed back into the stables. A few feet behind Miguel a man cleared his throat loudly.

"You don't think you were being a little too hard on them, do you?"

Miguel spun on his heel to see his old friend and the sheriff of Lincoln County, Roy Pardee. The sight of him lifted some of Miguel's sour mood, and with a half grin, he stepped forward and reached to shake the older man's hand.

"Not nearly as hard as I'm going to be if they don't shape up. I don't have time for whiners.''

"You said something about needing grooms. What's Chloe done now, bought more racing stock?''

Miguel shook his head. "Haven't you heard? She and Wyatt have gone off on a second honeymoon.''

Surprise crossed Roy's face. "That's news to me. I thought Adam had broken his leg and they'd gone to be with him.''

"They did. He's fine, so they decided to stay in South America and see the sights. Probably for a month.''

Roy rubbed his chin thoughtfully. "What about Anna? I thought she was back here visiting? In fact, that's why I stopped by. To say hello to her.''

As soon as Roy mentioned his niece's name, Miguel had the oddest urge to wipe the back of his hand against his mouth. He could still feel the imprint of her lips. Surely Roy could see it branded all over him.

"As of yesterday Anna has taken over the care of her mother's horses. And frankly I wish none of this was happening."

Roy shot him a puzzled look, then laughed. "What's the matter? Anna been shaking you up?"

Miguel frowned. "Shaking me up? How do you mean?"

Roy's laugh deepened, and Miguel was amazed to feel embarrassed heat fill his face.

"The last time I looked, Anna was mighty pretty."

Miguel shot him a disgusted glance. "I've seen pretty women before."

"Yeah. Years ago. I'm not sure you ever see any woman now. Much less one that looks like Anna."

Miguel jerked his thumb toward the stable behind him. "You'll probably find her in there."

Knowing his friend was deliberately putting an end to the subject, Roy grabbed him by the shoulder. "Good. Come along with me while I say hello."

"I have work to do."

"You always have work to do. It'll wait."

If it had been anyone other than Roy, Miguel would have told him exactly where to go. But Roy had been his friend for many years, ever since he'd worked as a deputy back in Albuquerque. He respected and admired him and cherished his friendship. He would not insult him over Anna.

The two men found her locking the chestnut away in his stall. The moment she spotted Roy, her face lit up with a joyous smile. She ran to him and flung herself into his arms.

"Uncle Roy! It's so wonderful to see you!" She

kissed his cheek, then kissed it again, making the sheriff laugh.

"Now that's the kind of greeting I like," he teased as he patted her back with a big, loving hand.

Anna pressed her cheek against his broad chest, then leaned her head back to look at him. "How's my favorite Texas Ranger?"

His expression full of amusement, Roy glanced over at Miguel. "How do you like that? She kisses me, then asks about my son."

"Charlie is my favorite cousin," Anna excused her behavior. "And I haven't seen him since his wedding to Violet."

"Charlie's fine. But you'd better not let your other cousins know he's your favorite or you'll have the whole bunch mad at you. Did you know Violet was expecting a baby?"

Anna nodded, while a few steps away Miguel was mesmerized by the sparkle in her eyes and the broad smile on her face. This was a totally different woman from the one he knew. This Anna was warm and giving. This Anna was hungry for the love and companionship of her family.

"Yes. Mother told me the good news. I'm so happy for them. When are they coming home? I'd love to see them while I'm here on the Bar M."

"Maybe the end of June," Roy told her. "Will you still be here then?"

The end of June was more than seven weeks away. Anna had only planned to stay on the ranch for six weeks, and one of those was nearly past.

Not daring to glance at Miguel, she said, "I don't know, Uncle Roy. I'm not sure about my concert schedule yet. But I'll try.'' She looped her arm through her uncle's. "Come on, let's go down to the house and I'll make you a cup of coffee.''

"Well, I was on my way home. But I guess Justine will wait a few more minutes. Besides, it worries her more when I come home early than it does when I'm late.'' He glanced at Miguel. "Come have coffee with us, Miguel. I'd like to hear how roundup is going.''

Miguel looked from the older man to Anna. The coolness he was accustomed to seeing was back on her face, and he felt a sharp slice of disappointment. He didn't want Anna's frost. He wanted her warmth.

"I have some things waiting—''

"Don't tell me you have things to do,'' Roy interrupted him. "There's always things to do on a ranch. I'm sure Anna makes good coffee. If she doesn't, we'll find some of Wyatt's brandy to pour in it.''

"Uncle Roy!'' Anna scolded teasingly. "I make delicious coffee. And sheriffs aren't allowed to drink.''

Laughing, Roy urged his niece out of the stables and motioned for Miguel to join them. Miguel felt he had little choice but to follow.

An hour passed before Roy eventually said his goodbyes and headed on home. Normally Miguel thoroughly enjoyed visiting with his old friend. But this evening he could hardly relax with Anna's presence filling the kitchen.

The more he tried not to notice her, the more he caught himself staring, recalling the kiss they'd exchanged at the stables.

Touching her had been a mistake. But when he'd walked up and seen her racing around the track on a horse even he would be leery to climb on, he'd been enraged. And he'd been frightened. Memories of Charlene's reckless indifference to his wishes had come rushing to his mind, filling him with helpless anger. Anna wasn't Charlene, but in Miguel's eyes, she was too damn close to the same mold.

"Miguel? Do you hear me?"

He glanced up to see Anna staring at him from across the room. "Did you say something?" he asked as he tried to shake away his deep thoughts.

"I asked if you were hungry. Do you want to stay and eat?"

Clapping his hat back onto his head, he rose from his seat at the table. "No. I've got things to do. I'll...see you in the morning."

Anna watched him head on out the door without giving her so much as a second glance. Well, that was the way she wanted him to be, she told herself. But her traitorous gaze flew to the windows and continued to watch him until his long strides carried him through the courtyard gate and out of her sight.

Miguel prepared himself a steak for supper, but he left half of it on the plate and refilled his wineglass instead. As he walked through the house, he couldn't ever remember feeling so restless.

He'd never been a man who needed much company other than his own. Usually he was content to switch on the television, prop his feet up and enjoy what was left of the evening before bedtime.

But tonight thoughts of Anna kept pestering him, refusing to let him do anything but think about her. He was attracted to her. He'd be a fool to try to convince himself he wasn't. Just looking at her was enough to make desire burn deep in his gut. Miguel knew firsthand what wanting a woman like Anna could do to a man. But he was beginning to think tonight he needed a reminder of the devastation.

Tossing off the last of his wine, he set the empty glass on a low coffee table and walked into his bedroom. In a desk wedged in one corner was a locked drawer. He opened it with a small key, then pulled out a heavy manila envelope.

The snapshots inside were all sizes. Some of them were clear, some fuzzy and many yellowed with time. He shuffled through them slowly, each one of them conjuring up a different memory. There was only one of the pompous wedding Charlene had insisted on. Miguel had wanted to be married in the same old church and by the same Catholic priest who'd baptized him as a child. But that would've been an insult to Charlene and her wealthy family, so Miguel had given in and endured a wedding in the Grant family mansion and a guest list of nameless people he'd never met in his life.

A tight grimace on his face, he tossed the photo to one side. He should have thrown it in with all the rest Charlene had taken after they'd divorced. The frozen image meant nothing to him now.

But there were many photos he did cherish like those of his parents and sister. And most of all there were those of his son, Carlos. The majority of them had been taken when he was a very young baby, before the divorce had separated them. Of course there were the yearly school photos right up to the sixth grade. But it was the early pictures of his son that Miguel related to the most. Back then he'd been able to see his son, to touch him, love him, father him. But that had all changed.

To look at Carlos as a sixth-grader, a soon-to-be teenager, both saddened him and reminded him why he could not let himself love Anna Sanders.

Anna had thought she was hungry, but by the time she'd eaten two thirds of her supper, her appetite had vanished, along with her determination to finish everything on her plate.

After scraping her plate, she cleaned off the countertop, then carried a cup of coffee with her into the living room. The house was as quiet as a tomb, and she tried to remember any other time she'd had the place to herself, but she couldn't think of one.

Instinctively she switched on the television, but after a quick run through the channels, she turned it off again. Eventually she wound up on the piano bench.

She was staring at the closed lid, wondering why she had no urge to play, when a voice suddenly sounded behind her.

Startled, her head whipped around, then a small breath rushed past her parted lips. "Miguel!"

"I didn't mean to frighten you," he said as he walked into the room. "I knocked at the kitchen door, but you didn't answer."

"Is something wrong?" she asked quickly.

As far as Miguel was concerned everything was wrong. He could not eat, sleep, rest or work without Anna intruding into his thoughts. Hell, tonight he hadn't even been able to stay in his own house. Something had drawn him back down here to the ranch house and her.

"No. I thought you might need help doctoring your hands." He knew it was a lame excuse for being here, but thankfully Anna didn't seem to notice.

She studied his face as he walked toward her. "I'm surprised you thought of my hands. You were pretty angry at me earlier."

Miguel couldn't help but notice she'd changed her dirty work-clothes for a printed gauze skirt and sleeveless sweater. Her long hair was collected with a huge barrette atop her head. The flame-colored curls spilled against her neck and brushed her delicate collarbones.

When he reached her, he couldn't stop his hands from closing around the mane of hair, tangling his fingers in the silken web of waves.

"I was angry," he admitted in a husky voice. "But that doesn't mean I want your hands to be neglected."

Even though Miguel had kissed her several times, on those occasions he'd always touched her out of provocation. Never had he reached out to her with such slow, deliberate intimacy as he was now. The feel of his fingers in her hair was flooding every inch of Anna's body with heat, stealing her breath and sending her heart into a mad gallop.

"I...uh, put some bandages on them after I got out of the shower," she murmured.

He eased down beside her on the piano bench and was suddenly consumed by the sweet scent of gardenia on her skin, the slight tremble of her lips as she met his gaze.

"Actually, I was already here before I thought of your bandages," he admitted. Then with a wry twist on his lips, he lifted one of her hands and opened the palm to his gaze. "I mainly come down to...tell you

I shouldn't have gotten so bent out of shape when I saw you on that horse. I was wrong to assume you didn't know how to handle him.''

Never in her wildest imaginings would Anna have ever dreamed of getting any sort of apology from this hard man. Much less one that seemed so genuinely sincere. And for once she didn't know what to think or say.

"For all you knew I'd never been on a racehorse before,'' she said, trying to meet him halfway. ''And I do understand, that, as foreman of this ranch, you feel responsible.''

Suddenly he chuckled softly, and Anna was shocked at how much she adored the sound of pleasure coming from his throat.

"After Roy left and I went home, I decided I was finally going to have to admit you are capable of doing more than play the piano.'' He shook his head, and the expression on his face went suddenly grave. ''But riding racehorses is very dangerous. I hope you realize just how dangerous.''

Her gaze searched his face for long moments, and her heart surged as she realized he was actually concerned for her safety and not just his job. The knowledge had her looking at him in a whole different light. ''Believe me, Miguel. I do know the dangers. I have a friend who's confined to a wheelchair because he fell on the track. It's not a job I take lightly. But for the next few weeks it is my job and I plan to do it as best and as safely as I can.''

He had to be satisfied with that. He had no right to say more. He was not Anna's husband, lover or even her friend. And even if he was, she was not the sort of woman to bend to a man's demands. And a part of Miguel admired her independence. The other part of him hated it. For more than a year he had tried to deal with Charlene's independence, and in the end he'd come to the realization that she would never really need him.

"Then I'll try to keep my mouth shut," he said.

Her eyes drifted to his lips, and like the ebb of the ocean, longing flooded through her, momentarily robbing her of breath. Of all the men she'd ever encountered, this one and only this one had the ability to make her forget everything. Her common sense, her morals, her vow to guard her heart from all men.

"Maybe I should put that down in writing," she said with a husky little laugh.

He smiled faintly, then to Anna's foolish disappointment he turned his gaze on the closed lid of the piano. "Are your hands too sore to play?"

She stared down at her hands and then at the old mahogany wood covering the keys. "I'm...not sure. I haven't tried."

Anna could feel his head turn slightly and his eyes glide over her profile. "Why not? I thought musicians had to play all the time to stay at their best."

"That's true. But this is my vacation. I don't want to practice."

The faint resentment he picked up in Anna's voice surprised Miguel. He'd figured all along the piano was her first love. Was she trying to imply it wasn't?

"What do you play?" he wanted to know. "Classical music?"

She nodded. "Sometimes. I can play most anything. Jazz, country and western, Broadway melodies and big band. I think big band—like the old Glenn Miller tunes—is my favorite.''

''Would you play something for me?''

For a moment her heart stopped, and her breath caught in her throat. Though she didn't understand why, she felt as if he'd just asked her to make love to him.

''I don't—'' She broke off with a hesitant shake of her head.

''Believe me, I won't notice if you make mistakes. Just play something you like. Something soft.'' Like you, he wanted to add, but didn't.

He could see the indecision behind her face, and he said nothing as he waited patiently for her to make up her mind. Finally she pushed up the lid and ran her fingers in a testing way over the keys.

''My parents bought this piano when I was only five,'' she told him in a wistful voice. ''It was old and cheap, but I loved it. Later after I learned to play pretty well, Daddy offered to buy me a baby grand. But I was already too attached to this one.''

Miguel would have never thought of her as being sentimental. But he was beginning to see he could not second-guess this woman. There were obviously layers of her he'd not yet seen. And he hated to admit just how badly he wanted to see and know all of her.

''If your blisters are too sore, forget about playing,'' he told her.

Anna glanced at him, and in that instant she knew it would give her joy to play for him and only him. It felt as though she had practiced and studied all these years just so she could give this man a few moments' pleasure.

Before she could analyze where her feelings were headed, she began to play a love song. Her fingers were stiff, but to a novice she played flawlessly, and the beautiful notes filled the room.

Once she was finished, Miguel sang a few snatches of the words, and Anna looked at him in surprise. "You know the song?"

A wry smile on his face, he said, "Yes. 'Night and Day.' Cole Porter wrote it back in the forties, didn't he?"

Impressed, she nodded, then with a shock of pink filling her cheeks, she admitted, "I didn't think you'd know it."

"I know very little about composers or lyricists. But I watch a few old classic movies from time to time. You pick up a lot about music from them." With a wry twist to his lips, he reached up and rubbed his forefinger against her heated cheek. "I don't think this blush is because you thought you affronted me, though. It's because you thought I didn't know you were playing me a love song."

Anna stared at the ivory keys, while beneath her breast her heart hammered erratically. "You said play something I like. So I did. I wasn't expecting you to know the words. Or to…read anything into them."

Miguel could feel her pulling away from him, the warmth he'd felt a few moments ago being replaced by cool indifference. Whether it was feigned or real, he didn't know. Nor did it really matter. She was telling him a love song from her would never be played in real life for a man like him.

With that sobering thought, he cleared his throat and

rose to his feet. "Don't worry, Anna. I would never make that mistake."

He moved away from the piano bench, and after a few moments Anna looked around to see he was gone. It was just as well, she tried to tell herself. But even as she did, her chin fell against her chest and hot tears oozed from her closed eyes.

She was falling in love with Miguel Chavez, she realized. A man who was bound to break her heart.

Chapter Six

Three days later Anna was coming into the house from the stables when the kitchen phone rang. Trying not to think about the nasty tracks her boots were leaving on the clean tile, she hurried across to the cabinets to answer it.

"Hi, sis! What's going on up there on the Bar M?"

Thrilled to hear her brothers voice, she squealed, "Adam! What are you doing? How's your leg?"

While he filled her in on his condition and his accident, Anna dragged up a chair, pushed off her dirty cowboy boots and made herself comfortable.

"Sounds like you were lucky your back wasn't broken," she said, once he paused for her reply. "So when are you coming home? Aren't you nearly finished down there?"

He clucked his tongue in a teasing way, and the sound reminded Anna of how Miguel had talked about Adam's sense of humor and her lack of one. Maybe he was right. Maybe she had forgotten how to really laugh.

"I'm just getting started. What's the matter, Annie? Missing your old twin brother?"

With the receiver cradled between her shoulder and her ear, she unwrapped the rubber band from the end of her braid. "I would like to see you. I was looking forward to us having some leisurely rides together. Without your hotshot," she added drily.

Her brother laughed. "You'll never let me live that down, will you?"

"Not a chance."

He laughed again, then asked, "How are you and the horses making it? Frankly, I thought Mom and Dad handed you a heavy load. But I guess they figured Miguel was there to help you."

Miguel. Adam couldn't know the horses were far easier to deal with than the unpredictable foreman. Since she'd played the piano for him the other night, he'd kept his distance and she hers. She hated the separation and hated the fact that she missed him, but she tried to tell herself it was all for the best.

"The horses and I are making it just fine," she assured him. "I'm not even saddle sore anymore."

"The city girl is back in the saddle again." He sang a line of the old Western song by a similar name, then finished it with a yodel that had Anna rolling her eyes with amusement. "Bet you're missing all those bright lights and applause."

"I've been too busy cleaning horse manure from under my fingernails to think about making music."

He made a scoffing of disbelief, then his voice grew more serious. "Are you really okay, sis? You know

Miguel will help you in any way. All you have to do is ask him.''

But she wouldn't ask him. So far she'd told the two inept cowhands what to do, and if they couldn't manage the job, she did it herself. ''Miguel has been busy with roundup.''

There was a long pause, and in spite of the thousands of miles separating them, Anna could feel her brother weighing her response like a sack of eggs.

''You haven't been home since Lester retired,'' he mused aloud. ''What do you think about Miguel?''

Anna closed her eyes. She wasn't ready to admit to herself that Miguel had gotten under her skin. Much less admit it to her brother.

''He seems a very capable man.''

Adam snorted at her answer. ''I know the man is capable, sis. I want to know what you think of him personally?''

''Why?''

He sighed. ''Because when I first mentioned his name you froze up.''

Anna groaned. ''I didn't freeze up! You can't see me. So you can hardly know what I'm doing back here!''

A long silence followed her outburst, then he said, ''You're getting hysterical now. Something must be going on between the two of you.''

Gripping the phone, she scooted up on the edge of the chair. ''Are you crazy? I hardly know the man!''

Anna expected Adam to continue his speculations, but he surprised her by suddenly switching gears. ''If that's the case,'' he told her, ''then you should get to know him. He's a great guy. And he's lonely. He could use your company.''

She tried to ignore the sudden wincing of her heart. "Mother says he dislikes women. And I am a woman," she reminded him drily.

"So. You might be able to make him see all women aren't like his wife."

Anna seized upon her brother's snippet of information. "You know his wife?"

"Only from what little he's told me about her. She sounded like a hellcat on wheels. I guess you know he has a son."

Everything inside Anna went completely still, and she stared at the receiver as though she was certain she'd heard wrong. "Did you say 'son'?"

"Yeah. I think he's about eleven or twelve now. Miguel doesn't say too much about him. But I can tell when he does talk about the boy, he really misses him. It's too bad he doesn't get to be with him."

"Doesn't Miguel see his son regularly?"

"He's been on the Bar M for more than a year now, and I've never seen the boy. And I don't think Miguel has gone back to Texas to see him. But I don't ask. I don't pry into the man's private business."

After that Adam moved their conversation on to other things, but Anna was mostly lost to what he was saying. Her mind was whirling with the knowledge that Miguel had a child. A son nearly twelve years old! Where was he, and why hadn't Miguel mentioned him to Anna?

Once Adam hung up with the promise to call again soon, Anna went to her bedroom and took a long, hot shower. By the time she was finished, she told herself she had to put Miguel out of her mind. It wasn't any of her business whether he had a son. But Adam's words wouldn't leave her alone. *Miguel is lonely. I can tell he misses the boy.*

Eventually she gave up fighting with herself and decided to take her brother's advice and give Miguel a little company. The most he could do was tell her to leave. If he did, she would go away and pretend it didn't matter to her one way or the other.

She dressed in a short-sleeved cotton sweater and a full skirt of Indian printed cotton. The copper, turquoise and burgundy shoes suited her, and along with her fiery hair gave her enough coloring to forgo makeup. The last thing she wanted was for Miguel to think she was going out of her way to entice him.

The evening before, Anna had made a green chili casserole and eaten very little of it. She pulled it from the refrigerator and carried it out to one of the pickup trucks she'd been driving on the ranch.

She was halfway up the mountain when she met Miguel coming down in his four-wheel-drive vehicle. The moment he spotted her, he pulled to the side of the narrow dirt road and waited for her to reach him.

"Where are you going?" he asked before she had a chance to say anything.

She stared. She'd never seen him so dressed up before. A clean gray felt was on his head and his white shirt was starched and sharply creased. His jaws were freshly shaven. The sight of him both thrilled and disappointed her. He was obviously going out.

"I was...coming up to see you." She glanced at the casserole on the seat beside her. Adam's phone call must have temporarily paralyzed her brain cells. She'd been an idiot for ever thinking Miguel might want or need her company.

"Is something wrong?" he asked.

"No. I…" She shrugged while wishing she'd never put herself in such an awkward position. "I thought you might not have eaten yet, and I have plenty of green chili casserole with me."

He studied her face, searching for a motive behind her suggestion. When her expression failed to tell him anything, he said, "Actually I was on my way into town to eat."

"Oh."

Sudden disappointment flickered in her eyes, and Miguel inwardly cursed. For the past three days she hadn't made any sort of effort to seek him out. It seemed suspicious as hell that she wanted to have a meal with him now.

"Why don't you tell me what you're really up to," he said.

His question stiffened Anna's backbone. "I'm not *up* to anything," she said coolly. "I was simply going to share my supper with you. But it's obvious you have other plans."

Not waiting for a reply, she gunned the motor, put the gear shift into low and pulled away from him.

Because the rocky lane was so narrow, she was forced to drive all the way to the honeymoon house to find a space wide enough to turn the truck around. By the time she headed back down the mountain, her face was still burning with humiliation.

It was a lesson well learned, she firmly told herself. Men were selfish, narrow-minded creatures. Scott had taught her that long before she'd ever come home to the Bar M. She needed to remember Miguel was no different from the rest of his gender.

She was still fuming, vowing never to make another friendly gesture to the man, when she topped a small rise and was suddenly faced with Miguel's Explorer parked smack-dab in the middle of the road.

Cursing out loud, she jammed on the brakes. Gravel spewed from all four tires as the truck skidded several feet on down the steep incline until it finally came to a halt half a foot away from his bumper.

Shaking with anger and fear, she jammed on the emergency brake and quickly climbed out of the truck. Miguel was already on the ground, waiting for her. "With that kind of driving, I hope your parents have their insurance paid up," he drawled mockingly.

Her mouth fell open, then snapped shut. "What are you doing? Trying to get this thing smashed?"

She gestured toward his vehicle, and Miguel could not miss the fire in her eyes. She was a beautiful woman. But even more so when anger flamed her cheeks and sparkled in her eyes. He had to admit he sometimes goaded her purposely, just to see the transformation.

"You left without saying goodbye. I thought I'd give you another chance."

His comment was so unexpected and ridiculous, she shook her head, then was unable to stop a small smile from tugging at her lips.

"You're crazy," she said to him.

With a lazy grin he watched the high-desert wind whip her hair like the flame of a piñon fire. "Would you like to drive into town and eat with me?"

The sight of his vehicle parked in the road had momentarily shocked Anna, but his invitation completely bowled her over.

"You don't have to pretend you'd like me to come along. I'd rather you be truthful with me."

That was the whole trouble, Miguel thought. He actually did want Anna to be with him. Though God only knew why. She was not a woman he should be letting into his life. But in this past week he had come to want her as he had wanted no other woman.

"If I didn't want you to come with me, I wouldn't have asked."

His face was shaded by the wide brim of his hat. Anna studied his passive expression for a few moments while she tried to decide what to do. She'd driven up here because she'd wanted to see him, to spend a little time with him and hopefully learn something more about his son.

Perhaps driving into Ruidoso with him would be even better, she thought. At least the two of them would be in a public place with no chance of anything physical happening between them.

"All right," she said finally, "I'll follow you down to the ranch house and leave my truck there."

Less than five minutes later Anna was sitting in Miguel's black Explorer. Dusk was falling but she was still able to watch the scenery fly by her windows as they headed away from the Bar M.

When he halted at a stop sign, then turned onto a two-lane asphalt highway, Anna realized it was the first time she'd been away from the ranch since she'd come home more than a week ago. She'd been so busy time had flown by, and she realized she had missed nothing of the outside world. Especially the time she used to spend at the piano or the long hours she endured traveling cross-country.

"I heard you finished roundup this evening," she said once he'd gone through the gears on the stick shift and the vehicle started to pick up speed.

"Who told you that?"

"One of the hands. Why didn't you tell me?"

The question hurt him nearly as badly as staying away from her had. "I've been busy. I didn't have time to come by the stables."

He was lying, and Anna knew she should let it rest. But she couldn't. His distance had puzzled her. All she'd done was play the piano for him, and he'd repaid her with indifference.

"If I'd known Cole Porter was going to put you in such a sour mood I would have played Beethoven," she said, trying to joke.

Miguel wished she hadn't brought up that night. He'd spent the past three days trying to forget how she'd looked and smelled, the beautiful music she'd made with her hands and most of all the longing he'd seen in her eyes. It had been all he could do to leave her and walk out of the house. After that he'd stayed away from her out of necessity. Even now he knew he shouldn't be with her like this. But she was a temptation he couldn't seem to resist.

"I've not been in a sour mood, Anna."

She glanced at his hard profile and was suddenly struck by how much pleasure it gave her to look at him, be with him. "So in other words you just haven't wanted to be around me."

He sighed. "I didn't say that. But now that you

have, I think we should be honest with each other. Just as you said a few moments ago.''

She continued to look at him as she waited for him to go on. He felt her gaze boring into the side of his face and was finally compelled to glance at her.

''We shouldn't be together,'' he said with a grimace. ''We bring out the worst in each other.''

Funny he should say that, Anna thought. The few moments she'd spent in his arms had been the very best of her life.

''I wonder why that is?'' she pondered quietly.

He shrugged. ''Because we're like fire and ice. One is bound to destroy the other.''

Anna's birth mother had destroyed nearly everything she touched. She'd had her chances at love and happiness but one by one she'd made a mess of them and subsequently her life. Anna was beginning to fear she was headed down the same destructive path. Especially when she looked at Miguel and wished for what could never be.

''Don't you think you're being a little overly dramatic?'' she asked him. ''We've had our differences, but we've gotten past them.''

''It's the way we get past them that worries me, Anna.''

She moved around in her seat. ''I don't know why it should worry you. It's not like Daddy is going to come home and force you into a shotgun wedding just because you kissed me.''

His nostrils flared at her glib remark. ''Maybe a few kisses don't mean anything to you. But to a man it's a green light. Pure and simple.''

The more he said, the worse she hurt. Deep inside

she wanted to believe something other than lust or anger had driven him to take her into his arms and taste her lips.

She sighed wearily. "Even though I've never slept with a man, I'm not ignorant of men or their behavior, Miguel. Six weeks ago I was planning to marry one."

His head jerked around in surprise. "You were engaged?"

She nodded while wondering why she'd let the admission slip past her lips. She hadn't been planning on telling Miguel about her broken engagement. What woman in their right mind wanted anyone to know she'd been cheated on?

"And making wedding plans," she answered grimly.

"What happened? You decided he wouldn't fit in with your career?"

"Not with another woman hanging on to his shirt-sleeve. Three is usually a crowd. Especially in a marriage."

He glanced at her sharply. "You're saying he was untrue?"

Her lips spread to a thin, mocking line. Thank God Scott's betrayal no longer hurt her, but it had taught her a hard lesson about men and fidelity. She'd have to be crazy or crazy in love to trust another one.

Refusing to be embarrassed, she lifted her chin. "When you walk in and see your betrothed in bed with another woman, the word for it isn't *untrue*. It's—" she broke off and waved her hand in a dismissive way "—it's bad. But it's survivable. I'm proof of that."

Miguel could not imagine such a thing happening

to Anna. She was a beautiful woman, and even though she was oftentimes remote and cool, he could see flashes of her passion trying to escape. How could any man ever look away from her and to another? She could give a man more than he could ever dream of. But passion wasn't everything, he quickly reminded himself. Charlene had certainly taught him that much.

"So unlike you, your fiancé wasn't choosy about his bed partner, so you've come back to the Bar M to mend a broken heart," he mused aloud.

Miguel should have known it was something like that and not just a vacation from her work. No wonder she'd kissed him with such abandon. She was probably on a giant rebound, looking for any man to soothe her feminine pride, and for some reason she'd picked him.

Anna primly crossed her legs and made sure her long skirt was down to her ankles. "My heart isn't broken. Now that my relationship with him is all in the past I don't think I ever really loved him. In fact, I'm quite glad to have him out of my life."

"Hell, you make him sound like an old dress you decided to throw away."

"On the contrary. I've had dresses I was fonder of than that...cheat."

Miguel recognized she had a right to be bitter. But he didn't like to think she could be as callous as Charlene, who'd tossed him away like an outdated garment she no longer wanted.

"The other day when Roy came by the ranch, I honestly got the notion you...cared about people. But now I'm beginning to wonder just who and what you care about."

She gritted her teeth and tried to slow her rocketing temper. "You think I don't have a heart just because I had the common sense to get over a man who was a liar and a cheat? Who do you think you're helping by pining after that ex-wife of yours? If she'd been any kind of woman at all you would have kept her, right?"

His eyes were little more than slits when he finally glanced at her. "What do you know about my ex-wife?"

"Nothing! Except that she must have been a bi—a difficult person. Or is that not true? Did the fault of your divorce lie with you? Is that why you never see your son?"

As soon as the questions were out, Anna was horrified at herself. She'd never meant to say them. At least not in such a blunt fashion. But he had such a way about him that one word, one glance was enough to rip away all her niceties.

Miguel's face grew rigid as a rock, then red, as he stared at the highway in front of them. "Who told you I had a son? Have some of the men been gossiping about me?"

Horrified with herself or not, another spurt of anger blasted through Anna, and she turned on him. "I'd hardly call it gossiping to say someone has a child! Or are you ashamed of him?"

With a brief glance in the rearview mirror, Miguel stomped on the brake and jerked the vehicle to the side of the highway.

Anna's heart was pounding as he killed the motor and deliberately turned in the seat to face her.

"I am not ashamed of my son! And you are never to speak of him again!"

"Why?" she dared to ask.

"Because he is none of your business!"

Anna's gaze was riveted to his face, and as she looked at him, she realized it was more than anger she was seeing. Her probing questions had ripped something away, exposed a vulnerable part of him he didn't want her to see, and the sight tore at her.

"No. I don't suppose he is my business. But he should be yours."

"What is that supposed to mean?"

"It means I had to find out about your son second-hand from my brother. That doesn't sound like a proud father to me!"

"Do you know how wrong, how ignorant it is of you to make insinuations about me? About my relationship with my son?"

His voice was low and furious, and Anna knew he wanted to strangle her. But for once she didn't care that she had angered him, that she had perhaps stepped over the line. She was doing it because she cared.

"Just like it was wrong of you to assume I was nothing but a musician," she shot back.

Her reminder hit home. After his eyes raked a few more cutting paths over her face, he sighed and settled back in his seat.

"Miguel, my intention wasn't to imply you were a bad father. I simply wanted to know about him. Why he isn't here with you," she said more gently.

He didn't reply. Anna sighed, then looked toward the window as the sting of tears touched the back of her eyes. "I guess I was a little hurt because...well, you obviously didn't want to share that part of your life with me.''

Long moments of silence continued to stretch inside the vehicle. Anna eventually turned her head to look at him. His anger was gone, and in its place she could see sad regret.

"Oh, Anna," he said softly. "It shouldn't matter to you. You getting tangled up in my life…it isn't good. For either of us. You'll be gone soon."

He was gently reminding her she had no place in his life or even a place on the Bar M, and she felt as if he'd stabbed her to the bone.

Glancing away from him so he couldn't see the glisten of moisture in her eyes, she said, "I might not be leaving soon. I might decide to stay here on the Bar M for good this time."

He muttered a curse under his breath. "You're talking silly now."

Anna's first instinct was to turn and scream at him. But the last thing she wanted was for him to add *hysterical* to her description.

As coolly and collectedly as she could manage, she said, "I don't think anyone is ridiculous for wanting to be home. If you do, I think you're the one who's heartless."

"That's not what I meant. I think it's crazy for you to consider giving up your career."

"You gave up yours," she countered.

He arched a brow at her. "I've never had a career."

"You were a lawman."

He grimaced. "I never intended to be a lawman for the rest of my life. But you have a talent. You'd never be happy if you gave it up. After a few months' time, you'd be frantic to get out of this place, to get back into a refined culture. And that's not even counting the money you'd be turning your back on.''

All her life Anna had heard those very words, and for years she'd believed she had no choice but to play music. Guilt had riddled her whenever the mere thought of giving it up flashed briefly through her mind. She didn't want to be a quitter, a loser like Belinda had been. But, dear God, she silently prayed, was she suppose to give up having a family, a home, all the things she'd ever wanted the most?

''It's always easy to give someone advice when you're looking through the other side of the fence.''

He sighed, reached for the ignition switch, then paused. ''I think you are a troubled girl, Anna. You don't know what you want.''

Two weeks ago she would have probably agreed with him. But now the once-confused vision in her heart was slowly growing clear. She wanted to be near Miguel. She wanted to feel his touch. She wanted to play for him. She wanted to wake with him each morning, look out over the mountains and know that she was truly home.

But how could she tell him how she was feeling? He didn't want her or any woman in that way. Even worse, he believed she was young and fickle.

''And you do?'' she countered softly.

His face closed, he reached for the ignition and the engine sprang to life. ''Right now I want my supper,'' he said brusquely. ''As for your question, that's my concern. Not yours.''

Was her brother out of his mind? *Miguel's a lonely*

man. He needs your company. Or was she the crazy one for listening to him in the first place?

"I'll try to remember that," she said flatly.

Supper was a quiet occasion. Miguel ate steak. Anna was contented with a shrimp salad. Their conversation touched on a few local happenings, the general condition of the ranch and some of the work they would both be doing in the next few days. But even though they talked, Anna felt a cold chasm stretching between them.

She didn't know if the awkward tension was because they'd said too much to each other or not enough. Whatever the case, she was relieved when he finally suggested they leave the restaurant.

On their way across the parking lot they passed a young couple heading toward the building. The man was leading a toddler while the woman was carrying a baby in a small carrier. Anna stared after them, her expression unknowingly wistful. Many of the friends with whom she'd grown up had already started families of their own. Violet was pregnant and Chloe had mentioned that Emily might be expecting again. But she could see no baby on her horizon. Not even the promise of one to come.

A few minutes later Miguel surprised her by saying, "You've gone quiet."

She shook away her thoughts and glanced at him. "I was just...thinking."

"Those people back in the parking lot, did you know them?"

She shook her head. "No. They...well, seeing them

made me wonder what it would be like to have children.''

He frowned skeptically. "Did you ever want children?"

Her head bent, her gaze on her lap, she nodded. "I've always wanted children."

"And how do you think a baby would fit in your life?" He didn't add the question of a husband. The idea of a man, any man making love to Anna, filling her with child was too repulsive for Miguel to consider.

"Just like anyone who has a baby," she answered. "They make a special place for him or her."

"And how could you be a mother?"

She lifted her head and looked at him with dark, wounded eyes. "You make me sound like a freak! Just because I entertain people for a living doesn't make me different from other women. I want the same things. Need the same things."

But her career did make her different, Miguel thought. And if she couldn't see that, she was headed for big trouble. "You've already had one broken engagement. You don't think your career had anything to do with that?"

"No. Scott had already agreed that I should tour until we started a family."

"Maybe he got tired of you being gone," he said, then shot her a knowing glance. "Men and children do require attention."

Anna started to lash back at him, but then suddenly noticed they were on a different road than the one they'd traveled into town.

She peered out the window. "Where are we... going?"

"You don't recognize where you are?"

She licked her lips as her heart began to pound with anticipation. "It's dark. And it's been a while since I traveled around Ruidoso."

"We're going up the mountain."

She jerked her head around, tried to find his expression in the darkness of the vehicle. "Sierra Blanca? Why?"

"Don't ask why. Just enjoy it."

It was a good thing Anna wasn't squeamish of heights. The narrow asphalt road climbing the mountain was drastically steep and nothing more than a maze of treacherous switchbacks. But Anna's thoughts weren't on the journey. She was too busy trying to figure out why Miguel was taking her to such a place.

At the top he parked, and the two of them climbed out to the ground. At twelve thousand feet, the night air was cold. Anna rubbed her hands over her bare arms as she joined him at the front of the vehicle.

"What are we doing up here?" she asked.

"Appreciating the view," he answered, then took her by the shoulder and guided her toward a paved area where one could safely look off the mountain.

Even though it was cold and she was at a total loss as to why she was standing atop Sierra Blanca, she still gasped with sheer pleasure and wonder as she gazed off into the valley of mountains stretched below them.

"Did you ever come up here in the winter and ski Apache?" he asked.

"Many times. I was never as good as my brother

or sister. Adam is very athletic and since Ivy is more petite than I she's more graceful on the snow. But I always managed to make it down the mountain without breaking my neck.'' She glanced at him. "Did you ever ski?''

He grunted with wry amusement. "No. Social sports were never my style. But Charlene loved it.''

"Charlene. Was that your wife?'' she ventured.

He nodded. "For a year and half.''

His admission completely stunned her. "Only for that long? Then you've obviously been divorced for a long time. How...why are you not able to forget her?'' she asked in a strained voice.

His roughly hewn profile turned, and his gaze found hers in the darkness. "You misunderstood me, Anna. I've forgotten Charlene a long time ago. Forgetting the pain she caused is another thing.''

"Tell me,'' she urged softly.

His hand moved up her shoulder to rest beneath her hair at the nape of her neck. "You're cold. We should be going.''

"I want to know,'' she said her gaze refusing to let his go.

His fingers pressed into her warm skin as he sighed and looked away. "Charlene was from a very rich and notable family in Albuquerque. I met her at a charity function put on by the sheriff's department. She was beautiful and flashy, and I suppose it was flattering to a young struggling deputy to be pursued by a woman like her. But I married her because I thought she loved me. Because I thought I loved her. Yet it took me only a few months to figure our marriage was...not much more than an adventure to her. After the novelty of being married to a real cowboy deputy wore off, she wanted her freedom.''

Horrified, Anna shook her head. "But if she had your son, surely she must have taken your marriage seriously.''

His face was suddenly carved from stone, and the caustic laugh that erupted from his lips chilled Anna far more than the mountain air.

"Charlene was furious when she discovered she was pregnant. I had to beg, cajole, do everything I could think of to prevent her from getting an abortion. She wanted a divorce, and I wanted my child. It was the only bargaining power I had.''

Anna's heart ached for all he'd gone through and lost. And ached, too, for the chance to take away his pain and bitterness. "What happened after your son was born?''

"After Carlos was born, Charlene's motherly instincts must have kicked in because she made a complete turnaround. She wanted her son. She also still wanted a divorce.''

"Did you try to fight for custody?''

He nodded gravely. "At first I fought hard. But Charlene's father was councilman for the city of Albuquerque and big buddies with most of the judges. Besides that, her family had enough money to keep me in court forever.'' He shrugged with weary acceptance. "In the end I gave Carlos up, because I knew they could give him so much more than I ever could. Since then Charlene has remarried, and thankfully her life is settled now. Her husband is good to Carlos and treats him as his own.''

Anna turned to face him, and her palm found the

middle of his warm chest, the rapid thud of his heart. "But you are his father, Miguel. Don't you think he needs you?"

His eyes blinked, his throat worked to swallow, and then his fingers lifted and gently brushed across her cheek. "Nobody has ever needed me, Anna. Nobody."

Chapter Seven

Anna knew a crippled horse when she saw one. Although the limp in his right foreleg was slight, the swelling around his hoof and fetlock were marked enough to worry her.

She motioned at the newly trained groom who was leading the horse around in a small circle so Anna could observe his gait.

"That's enough, Dale. Put him back in his stall."

"You want me and Sam to rub it with liniment or something?" the young man asked.

Anna shook her head. "No. I'm not sure what's wrong. I don't want to start any treatment until I have someone look at him. Do you know whether Mr. Chavez has been down here to the ranch yard yet this morning?"

"Yes, ma'am. He's already come and gone. Him and another hand went over to Roswell to see about a load of alfalfa."

So that meant he wouldn't be back at the ranch for several hours, Anna calculated. She would have preferred to have his opinion about the horse's foot before summoning a vet. He knew horses inside and out, and he could possibly advise her on how to care for this one, but she dare not wait until he got back to the ranch. The animal was one of Chloe's best runners. She didn't want to take the chance of postponing treatment. His condition might grow worse.

A week had passed since she and Miguel had gone into Ruidoso for supper. Since then Anna hadn't pushed her company on him, and he'd more or less stayed out of her way. Because he felt that was the safe thing for him to do, she supposed. But his revelations that night had told her much. Now when she looked at Miguel she knew he wasn't just a hard, arrogant man who preferred his own company. He'd been wounded by a callous woman. He couldn't forget his broken marriage because he still had a son somewhere out there whom he loved and missed. Anna figured until he'd made a steady, concrete connection with the boy, he would continue to hang on to the bitter past.

She wasn't at all sure what she could do about Miguel or even if she should do anything. She tried to tell herself he was right about them being like ice and fire. Maybe they were no good for each other. Maybe he would never love her. But she couldn't ignore the way her heart throbbed at the very sight of him, or the pure joy she felt whenever he was near. She loved the man. She couldn't let him go without a fight.

At the ranch house she located the name and number of the veterinarian her mother normally used. Unfortunately he was out for the day so she tried the second number her mother had jotted down as an alternative. After a quick discussion with his receptionist, Anna learned he was tied up for the morning, but he could come to the ranch later that afternoon. Anna assured the woman she'd be waiting.

"What the hell is he doing here?" Miguel mouthed out loud as he pulled the pickup to a stop a few yards away from the stables.

Elmer, the old wrangler sitting next to Miguel, glanced at his boss then out the window at the young veterinarian standing with Anna in the open doorway of the building.

"Guess the missus needed a doctor."

Miguel snorted. "She doesn't need his kind of doctoring."

Elmer strained to keep a grin off his face. "Chloe says he'll do in a pinch."

"He might know about animals, but not about women. I'll bet he's spent five minutes doing his job and another forty-five talking to Anna."

"Hmm. Well, I don't hardly see anything wrong with that. Miss Anna's probably lonely with all her family being gone."

Miguel gave the man an odd look, but said nothing. He didn't want to sound jealous. Because he wasn't, he assured himself. He just didn't want Dr. Dalton getting chummy with Anna. The man was known for his philandering, and she'd already been hurt by a man with a roaming eye.

But as Miguel got out of the truck and walked over to the two of them, he had to fight the urge to take the veterinarian by the collar and boot him off the Bar M. He didn't want this man or any man looking at Anna in a possessive way!

Anna didn't miss the dark look on Miguel's face as he approached her and the doctor. She didn't know what could be on his mind, but from the expression on his face she figured it had to be her. She seemed to be the only one or thing that could rile him.

"Miguel, have you met Dr. Dalton?" she asked.

He nodded coolly at her and the young, blond vet. The man was tall and slim with a walrus mustache that drooped around his mouth. Miguel couldn't help but wonder if she thought him handsome. She'd certainly been smiling at the doctor a moment ago when he and Elmer had driven up.

"We've met."

Anna frowned at his brusque response. "One of the horses is lame. You were gone, so I thought I'd better have Dr. Dalton look at him."

"And what did he find?" Miguel asked her, rather than acknowledge the vet.

"He's afraid it might be a hairline fracture. I'm going to need to drive him in for an X ray tomorrow."

Miguel's narrowed eyes darted over to the other man. "Why don't you take the horse back with you now and save Anna a trip into Ruidoso? You have your stock trailer with you."

He shrugged in a noncommittal way and tugged uncomfortably at the brim of his straw hat. "I'd rather not put the horse in my trailer. I've had some distempered animals in it this morning."

Miguel's face grew so dark, Anna actually believed he was going to explode.

"Then get it the hell out of here!" he practically shouted. "And I'll tell you another thing, Dalton. If one of Anna's horses so much as sneezes I'm going to hold you personally responsible!"

Anna watched the young vet open his mouth to defend himself, but then he must have decided a quick exit would be the best recourse. He snapped his mouth shut and stalked off to his pickup.

After he'd started the engine and pulled away, Anna whirled on Miguel. "What do you think you're doing!"

"Trying to save Chloe's horses. The damn idiot! What did he think he was doing coming out here with an infected trailer?"

"Maybe he's disinfected it before he drove out here and simply wanted to be extra careful," she reasoned.

He rolled his eyes with disbelief. "Maybe you should have been paying more attention to it than him. The thing was full of horse manure!"

Anna flushed. She hadn't noticed the nasty condition of the trailer. But Miguel needn't be so smug about it.

"Okay. So he shouldn't have been up here spreading germs. You didn't have to talk to him like he was...a piece of trash."

"As far as I'm concerned that's just what he is."

Anna gasped. Then before she could respond, Miguel turned and stalked off into the stables. Stunned, she stared at the spot where he'd disappeared, then anger propelled her to race into the barn after him.

"What is that suppose to mean?" she hurled at him once she'd gotten within earshot of his back.

Not pausing in his stride, he continued on toward

the tack room. "Just what I said. And tomorrow you'll not take that horse in by yourself. I'll be going with you!"

She grabbed him by the arm and forced him to stop and face her. "Why?"

His eyes took the time to roam her face. Bright color burned across her cheeks, and her green eyes were sparking like burning piñon. Miguel fought desperately with himself to keep from taking her into his arms and kissing her breathless. He wanted to possess her body and soul. But to do so would be asking for a heartache far worse than Charlene had ever caused him. "Because I don't want you to be alone with him."

Anna's lips parted as she stared at him in stunned wonderment. "Are you…jealous, Miguel?"

His nostrils flared. "No! I simply don't want Chloe coming home and finding her daughter mixed up with a man like him."

Anna didn't know what sort of man Dr. Dalton was. She really didn't care. All she wanted was her horse's ailment tended to. And as for her getting mixed up with a man. She already was. With him. Didn't he realize that? Or did he just not want to?

"You really think I'm a silly nitwit, don't you? You have this notion if someone wasn't around to tell me what to do, I wouldn't know how to take care of myself."

"I'm beginning to wonder if you do," he snapped. "Thirty more minutes and you'd have probably been making a date with Dr. Dalton. And this from a woman I heard swearing off men forever!" he added nastily.

Fury turned her face scarlet. "You don't know what you're talking about! Dr. Dalton and I discussed nothing but my horses. And even if we had discussed more, why should you care? You don't want me!"

It was all the goading Miguel could take. Grabbing her by the shoulders, he pulled her to within an inch of him.

"You don't know what wanting is, Anna," he growled. "You—"

The rest of his words lodged somewhere in his throat as she suddenly pressed herself against him and grabbed his face between her palms. "And you think you do?" she whispered, her lips hovering a breath away from his. "If you did, you would know how I'm feeling right now. How I feel every time I look at you."

Heartbreak or not, Miguel could not withstand her or the white-hot desire pounding through him like a pagan war dance.

"You shouldn't be saying such things to me, Anna," he whispered roughly. "And I shouldn't be listening."

She closed the minute space between their lips, and he was helpless to resist. He stood motionless, his hands gripping her shoulders tightly as she tasted, searched the hard contours of his mouth. It was both heaven and hell to let her kiss him. And he was trembling with a need as old as time when she finally pulled her head away from his, shook back her tumbled hair and caught his eyes with hers.

"You think I'm young and foolish. You think deep down that all I'll ever want is to play the piano for a crowd of people, to travel in the glittering world of entertainment. But that isn't what I want, Miguel. I want you.''

Hearing her say the words left him feeling naked and more exposed than he ever had in his life. Because he was sure if she looked, really looked inside him she would see just how deep and wide his desire for her had grown.

He glanced away from her and drew in a ragged breath. He couldn't lose himself to this woman. Charlene had stomped his heart. Now so little of it was capable of feeling, loving. If Anna went away, and she would surely go, the last of himself would go with her and he'd be a ruined man.

''We don't always want what we need, Anna. You'll realize that...when you get older...and away from here.''

She wanted to ask him what he needed. If not her, then his son? But at that moment two men noisily entered the opposite end of the long barn and they were forced to break apart.

Anna turned her back to him, breathed deeply and tried to compose her scattered senses. She hadn't really meant to throw herself at Miguel like she had. She hadn't planned to actually tell him in words how she wanted him. But in the heat of the moment her feelings had burst from her. Now she couldn't hide from herself or him.

''I'm not sure what's wrong with the horse,'' she said, deliberately getting back to the point at hand. ''If you would, I'd like for you to look at him and give me your opinion.''

''Why bother with my opinion now? You've already called in a professional.''

She turned back to him, her expression full of disbelief. "Surely you can't fault me for that! It would be negligent of me to take risks with one of Mother's best runners!"

Miguel knew his jealousy was unreasonable. He had no right to throw such accusations at her. But his heart was already forming the idea that she belonged to him, and he didn't have a clue as to how to stop it.

Heaving out a heavy breath, he said in a gentler tone, "I'll take a look at the horse, Anna. But you need to remember I haven't had eight years of medical schooling like Dalton."

She turned to him and smiled as though he'd just plucked a star from the sky and presented it to her on a silver platter. "No. You've had many more years of experience. In my opinion that counts for much more."

Miguel had never felt he had an ego. Especially one that needed to be fed. But Anna's words swelled his chest with a strange sort of pride.

"Come on. He's down here at the end of the barn," she invited, then turned and headed down the wide alleyway covered ankle-deep in clean wood shavings.

Miguel followed and joined her in the horse's stall.

"I haven't done anything different with him," she said. "Yesterday I took him around the track a couple of times. He never so much as stumbled, and later, on the walker, his gait was fine. But this morning his ankle is swollen and he's limping noticeably."

Miguel approached the brown horse with gentle words of greeting, then after a few pats on the nose and neck to let him know he was a friend, Miguel lifted the horse's ailing foot.

He examined the bottom of the hoof, then slipping a small knife from his jeans pocket, he gently tapped it against the metal shoe. The horse immediately flinched and tried to jerk his foot away from Miguel's grasp.

Miguel looked up at Anna who was hovering a step away. A worried expression marred her face. "When was this horse last shod?" he asked her. "These shoes look new."

"I—" She shook her head as she tried to remember exactly. "The farrier has been here twice since my parents left. I think he shod this horse yesterday afternoon. Yes, I'm sure of it now. He'd already been exercised."

Still holding on to the horse's hoof, he nodded grimly. "I think his hoof has been cut back too short or he's been quicked with a nail. Get me a pair of pliers from the tack room. This shoe needs to come off."

Anna hurried after the tool, then back in the stall she watched Miguel carefully pry the shoe with its running cleat off the horse's hoof.

"See this," he told her pointing out one of the nail holes. "The farrier missed the wall and went into the sole. From the looks of this drainage it's already infected."

"Oh, my! I'm so glad you found it, Miguel. The poor animal was in misery! Why didn't Dr. Dalton have the foresight to remove the shoe?"

Because he'd been too busy looking at you, Miguel thought, but kept the opinion to himself. He'd already shown too much of the green monster inside him. He lowered the horse's hoof to the ground.

"The vet told me he believed the horse might have a hairline fracture or a torn ligament!" Anna exclaimed without waiting for his reply. "Now I won't have to haul him into Ruidoso tomorrow for X rays."

"Yes you will. The horse still needs treatment."

"Just tell me what to do to him," she said.

Anna's confidence in him was something he'd never expected, and he was overwhelmed at the pleasure it gave him. Charlene had never thought him clever or admirable. She'd simply liked the way he looked in a pair of jeans and cowboy hat. She'd never bothered to find out what was underneath. She hadn't cared what was underneath, he thought bitterly.

"It's—" He cleared his throat as his voice threatened to go husky with emotion. "I could tell you a few things to do. But I prefer you take him into the vet. The horse will probably need to be prescribed antibiotics. I can't do that."

She stuffed her hands into the front pockets of her jeans. "When can you go with me?"

He looked at her sheepishly. "I'm not going."

Anna's mouth popped open. "But you said…"

"Forget what I said. I was out of line."

His gaze fell to his boots, and Anna studied his downcast face. If he'd felt a streak of jealousy over her earlier, he was obviously regretting it now.

"I've grown used to you getting out of line," she said with as much teasing humor as she could. "I'd think you were sick if you weren't trying to boss me."

He couldn't think of any other time Anna had teased him or smiled at him in just the way she was doing now. And though he wanted to be cool and unaffected, he was actually floundering like a lost goose.

Miguel knew, just as Anna knew, that in the past few minutes things had forever changed between them. No matter what happened in the future, he would never be able to look at her again without feeling her hands upon his face, her lips pressed to his, her voice whispering she wanted him.

"I'll see you when you get back tomorrow," he said abruptly, then left the stall without giving her the chance to argue. Or provoke him into another kiss.

The next day it was nearly noon by the time Anna drove the lame horse into Ruidoso, waited for Dr. Dalton to examine him, then drive back to the Bar M.

Driving up the lane to the ranch, she glanced grimly at the sack of medicine on the seat beside her. There was a bottle of liquid antibiotics to be injected, plus a solution to spray on the wound itself. The doctor had appeared a bit annoyed that Miguel had taken it upon himself to remove the horse's shoe and make his own diagnosis, but in the end the veterinarian had agreed, albeit reluctantly, the foreman was correct. Anna could see he'd been embarrassed by his own oversight.

At the ranch, she was surprised when she pulled down to the stables and parked. Her cousin Emily and little second cousin Harlan walked out of the building to greet her. Even more amazing was to see Miguel a step behind the two of them. But then she should have known the man knew her family better than she did.

"Anna!" Emily exclaimed as she fiercely hugged her cousin. "Every time I see you you've grown more gorgeous!"

This was the first Anna had seen her older cousin since she'd come home last Valentine's Day for Charlie's wedding to Violet. Little Harlan had only been a newborn then. Now he was a chunky toddler, and Emily looked radiant with happiness. Anna was thrilled for her cousin. She'd suffered through many hard years before she'd been reunited with her true love.

Laughing, Anna gestured to her dusty jeans and plaid work shirt. "Oh, I'm sure I look good like this! But thanks for the compliment, anyway."

"Miguel tells me you have a lame racehorse. Does your mother know about him yet?"

Anna nodded. "I told her last night when she called." She glanced at Miguel, who'd yet to say anything. "She says as long as she knows Miguel is keeping an eye on him, she won't worry."

"Chloe's confidence is misplaced," Miguel spoke up. "Anna is quite capable of seeing after the horse."

His remark floored Anna, but Emily seemed to accept it as genuine.

"Well, I'm just glad Chloe's not fretting," the older woman said. "I'd hate for her vacation to be ruined. I can't ever remember her taking off like this. Wyatt makes business trips at times, but your mother rarely leaves the ranch. She was due for a break." She arched a brow at Anna. "What about you? How does it feel being home again?"

"It feels wonderful," Anna said, and then realizing how very much she meant it, she knelt down to greet Harlan. He had pale blond hair and blue eyes like his mother. At the moment one hand was clinging to a fold in the leg of her jeans, the other went straight to his mouth where he immediately began to chew on his forefingers as he studied Anna carefully.

"Hi, Harlan," she spoke gently to the child. "I'm

your second cousin, Anna. Are you saying words yet? Can you say Mama or Dada?''

The toddler continued to look Anna over, then glanced at Miguel and finally his mother to make sure the woman kneeling in front of him was acceptable. Once he decided she was safe, he pointed a finger over her shoulder and blurted, ''Horse!''

Anna laughed heartily while Emily made a helpless gesture with her hands. ''What can I say, it's in his genes.''

''Do you like to ride a horse, Harlan?'' Anna asked the child.

He pointed eagerly again to the pen behind her, which was filled with working cow ponies. Emily said in a hushed tone to Anna. ''Don't get him started. Once he gets on a horse, you can't get him off.''

Laughing again, Anna smiled at the boy, then patted his rotund little tummy. ''You just wait, Harlan. When you get a bit bigger, you can ride with me all day long.''

Emily groaned with fond humor. ''That's right. Be just like Coop and spoil him rotten. I'll pay you back when you have a child, Anna.''

Feeling like an interloper, Miguel slipped away while the two women continued to visit. As it had before, the sight of Anna with her family bothered him. Especially the sight of her with little Harlan. He didn't want to picture her as a warm, loving mother. It was easier to think she'd never fit the role. But the adoration in her eyes for Emily's child was already stuck in his mind. Along with many other things he didn't know how to forget.

At Anna's truck and tailer, he unloaded the lame

horse, put him back in his stall and placed the anti-
biotic in a small refrigerator in the tack room. As for
discussing the animal's treatment with Anna, he decided he could do that later after her cousin went
home. He had plenty of work to do himself, and anything to get Anna out of his mind would be a relief.

Outside the north end of the stables, the two women
continued to catch up on their family news. Until Emily looked around in sudden horror.

"Where's Harlan? He was standing right here beside us just a minute ago!"

"I don't know! I didn't see him move away," Anna
exclaimed.

Both women spotted the child at the same moment.
Emily screamed and Anna gasped with sheer terror.
The toddler had wandered past the pen of cow ponies,
then crawled beneath the metal rail fence and into another holding pen where a stallion had been let loose
to exercise. The animal was huge in size and possessed
a testy disposition. Anna had no idea how he might
react to the child.

Anna and Emily raced toward the baby at the same
time the stallion noticed the little intruder inside his
domain.

"Harlan! Harlan come to Mommy!" Emily
shouted.

The frantic tone of his mother's voice only frightened Harlan. The baby stopped in his tracks and began
to cry in earnest. Behind the baby, the stallion began
to paw the ground and snort.

There were two fences separating the women from
the toddler. They both climbed as fast as they could,
but Anna had the horrible fear they would never reach

the baby in time. Then out of nowhere she heard Miguel shouting for them to get out of the way. He flew past her and Emily and leaped into the holding pen just as the stallion started to charge.

Both Emily and Anna watched in stunned horror as Miguel threw himself between the baby and the vicious horse. With his back to the stallion, he scooped Harlan protectively against his chest.

Then everything seemed to happen in slow motion. The animal reared on his hind legs, then brought down both front hooves against Miguel's upper back. The force of the horse's blow staggered Miguel. He went to his knees, but somehow managed to hold on to the baby.

By the time the two women clambered to the ground inside the pen, the stallion had reared and struck Miguel a second time, then trotted away to one corner where he nervously pranced, snorted and tossed his head.

Emily snatched her son into her arms and quickly inspected him for injuries. Anna grabbed Miguel's arm as he lurched forward like a drunk man.

"Miguel! You're hurt!"

"The baby—"

Anna glanced at Emily who was nodding with relief. "He's fine, Miguel. But you're not!"

"Can't...breathe. I..."

If Anna hadn't been holding on to him he would have fallen in the dirt rather than into the circle of her arms. As she tried to support his sagging weight, she looked frantically at Emily.

"Go call 911!"

With Harlan clutched safely in her arms, Emily raced off toward the house.

"The stallion..." Miguel wheezed through clenched teeth.

"I'll take care of him," she said firmly.

He shook his head as his fingers bit into the flesh of her arm. "Get out...before he hurts you!"

She couldn't believe he was concerned about her safety when it was all he could do to keep from collapsing. "Can you make it to the fence?"

"Try," he gasped.

The pallor on his face and his struggle for breath terrified Anna, but for the moment she tried not to think about how badly he might be injured. She had to concentrate on getting him away from the dangerous horse and to medical care.

By the time she half dragged Miguel to the corner of the pen, he was on the verge of passing out. She didn't want to leave him for a second, but from the corner of her eye, she could see the stallion was charging up for another attack.

The animal didn't like anyone in his territory. But most often he accepted it. Anna had never seen him behave so viciously, and she feared if she didn't do something and fast, he would paw Miguel again.

All the cowhands were out vaccinating cattle in one of the back pastures. She'd sent the two grooms to Alamogordo to fetch a mended saddle from a tack shop. There was no one but her to save Miguel.

Her mind spun as her eyes darted around the pen. How was she going to get the animal out of there without him hurting her, too? And then she spotted a coiled lariat resting atop a fence post. She made a dash for the rope and quickly built a large loop. A few yards away, the black stallion began trotting back and forth and shaking his head from side to side.

Slowly, with the lariat rope held close to her side, she began to inch nearer the animal. He rolled his eyes, snorted, then kicked out with both back feet. Hooves slammed furiously against the metal fencing. The pipe clattered loudly but thankfully held together.

With her heart beating in her throat, Anna moved closer still. The horse pinned his ears, bared his teeth and charged. Anna stood her ground until the horse was almost to her, then quickly sidestepped his path at the last moment. He ran on past her, giving her enough time to whirl the loop open above her head. When the horse turned and headed back in her direction, she was ready. With the flip of her wrist, she threw a backward loop that settled neatly over the horse's head.

She pulled the slack and dug in the heels of her cowboy boots at the same time. The power of the horse jerked her off her feet, and she landed in a belly flop against the hard ground, but somehow she managed to hold on to the lariat. The horse began to drag her as she gripped the rope with all her might, refusing to give up. The hard nylon slipped through her hands taking skin, blood and flesh with it.

Just when Anna thought she couldn't stand the searing pain another second, the horse stopped. Dazed with fear and exertion, she rose to her feet, then stumbled over to the nearest fence post and whipped the rope around the rail.

Once she had the horse safely tied, she hurried over to Miguel and sank to her knees beside his crumpled form. His face was still deathly gray, and his breathing was so shallow she feared it was going to stop altogether.

"Miguel! The paramedics are coming. We'll get you to the hospital soon," she said to assure him.

He groaned and attempted to speak.

"The...stallion.. You...roped...him."

Anna cradled his head in her lap and smiled tearfully down at him. "I had to, darling," she whispered shakily. "He was going to hurt you again."

Miguel opened his mouth to speak again. He wanted to tell her how very brave and very foolish she was. He wanted to tell her she'd saved his life. But he couldn't find the strength to form the words.

His eyes tried to talk, and they must have conveyed something to her because she smiled down at him again. She spoke softly, but the roaring in his head drowned out her words. He felt her bloody hand press tenderly against the side of his face, and then everything went black.

Chapter Eight

When Miguel woke later that night, he was wrapped in pain and totally disoriented. There was no bright sky above his head or desert wind on his face. Instead of pine and sage, the air was stale and faintly scented with disinfectant.

With great effort he slowly forced his heavy eyelids open. The room was in semidarkness, but as his eyes grew accustomed to the subdued light, he recognized he was in a medical facility. Two intravenous tubes were stuck in his arm, and just to the left of the bed some sort of monitor beeped to the rhythm of his heart.

His first inclination was to raise himself up, but the excruciating pain stabbed him like a thousand knife blades. He groaned out loud and fell limply back against the pillow.

From a chair in the corner of the small room, Anna heard him and hurried to the side of the bed.

"Miguel! You're finally awake." She clicked on a small light over the top of his head.

He looked up at her and realized there was nothing he'd rather see at this moment than Anna's face. He tried to speak, but his mouth was like a dry arroyo. He swallowed and tried again. "What's the matter with me? I feel like a trussed-up turkey."

His voice was groggy from the painkillers they'd given him earlier, but Anna was certain she'd never heard a lovelier sound. "Several of your ribs were broken. One punctured your lung. But the doctor says you're going to be fine now."

Anna didn't go on to tell him just how serious his condition had been by the time they'd gotten him to the emergency room. There was plenty of time for that later. She didn't want to worry him needlessly.

Fractured images began to race through Miguel's mind. The stallion rearing on his legs, baby Harlan crying and Anna being drug on the end of a rope. "Is little Harlan okay?"

"He's fine, thanks to you."

Her answer filled him with relief. "When can I get out of here."

"The doctor says in a few days. If you progress well."

He looked incredulous. "I can't stay here a few days," he said with as much force as he could muster under the circumstances. "I have work to do."

"The only work you have now is getting those ribs mended back together," she told him. "The ranch will be taken care of until that happens."

He frowned at her skeptically. "Don't tell me you're going to take care of everything."

She shook her head and smiled at him. "Only part of it. Uncle Harlan is going to take over for you. By the way, the whole family is out in the waiting room. They'll be happy to hear you've come around.''

He was overwhelmed, and it showed on his face. "They're in the waiting room? But why?"

It struck Anna then just how completely alone this man believed he was, and it tore a hole right in her heart. "Because," she said softly, "they all care about you. And Emily and Cooper want to thank you for saving their baby.''

"I didn't—"

"Don't try to act humble, Miguel. If you hadn't grabbed little Harlan and put yourself between him and that stallion there's no telling what might have happened. One blow from his hoof would have killed the baby!" It almost killed you, she very nearly added.

Miguel's gaze dropped to the white sheet covering his chest. "I only did what I would have done to save my own boy.''

His own boy. Anna had not forgotten, even for a moment, about Miguel's son. Now she could only think about a twelve-year-old boy out there somewhere who had no idea his father was a brave hero or that he was hurt and in the hospital. It was incredibly sad to think about, and she had to look away and swallow the burning lump in her throat.

"I know. You would do it for any child," she said huskily. Then, looking back at him, she added, "Do you have any idea why the stallion went so berserk? He's been on the ranch since I was a teenager. He's certainly always been an animal you have to be cautious around, but I've never seen him become so vicious.''

Miguel grimaced. "Sometimes it's hard to say what

makes an animal suddenly switch gears. Most stallions are volatile. But as for this one, I don't know. Little Harlan's crying might have scared or disturbed him."

Anna shook her head and shuddered at the awful memory. "Well, whatever the reason, the horse is going to be sold at auction Friday."

He stared at her. "Under whose authority?"

"My mother's. She's already been contacted about your accident. She says she's not about to chance the horse hurting someone else."

"He's sired some wonderful offspring. I hate to see him go."

"I don't. I hate him for what he did to you."

Her words had him taking a second look at her. She was pale; her undereyes shadowed with fatigue. He wondered how long she'd been sitting in the room with him, and what her family must be thinking about her being here.

"He could have killed you, Anna! He was dragging you, and you wouldn't let go!"

"I couldn't let go, Miguel. He would have trampled you or both of us."

She brought her hand up and brushed at the limp black curl lying against his forehead. It was then Miguel realized her hands were bandaged. He caught the one nearest his face and studied the thick pad of bandages on her palms and fingers.

"I'm glad I can't see the damage beneath these things," he muttered grimly. "That was a crazy thing you did. Now your hands—your playing—"

She placed a fingertip against his lips. "My hands will be fine."

But if they weren't, would she blame him? he wondered. No. Anna would never blame him for such a thing. He was beginning to see she was not that sort of selfish woman. She'd risked her own life to save his. And that was very nearly too much for his heart to comprehend.

"If I thought you couldn't play anymore because of me—" He winced as he tried to draw in a deep breath. "I couldn't live with that, Anna."

Her green eyes were soft as she laid her hand on his shoulder. "You're talking too much. You should be resting. I'm going to go let the nurse know you're awake. You might be needing more painkiller."

He needed her, Miguel thought. Much more than any drug. She eased the pain in his heart, where he hurt the most. But he wasn't a fool. He realized she would be far more addictive than a drug, and in the end much harder to get and keep.

She leaned forward to get up and he caught her fingers gently with his. His thumb rubbed the edges of the adhesive, fastened to the back of her hand. "Is your family really out there?" he asked.

The fact that he had any doubts filled Anna with such sorrow that tears stung the backs of her eyes. "Yes. They are. Rose and Harlan. Roy and Justine. Emily and Cooper. Emily is especially distraught because you were hurt. She feels guilty because little Harlan managed to slip away from her."

He shook his head. "It would be hard to find a better mother than Emily. Little ones can get away in the blink of an eye."

"Did you know she and Cooper are expecting another baby?"

The look of surprise on his face answered her question. "That's good," he said. "That's as it should be."

And the way it should be with him and her, Anna thought, but she kept the notion to herself. Miguel had to get well before she could convince him he, too, had a right to happiness.

By the end of the week Miguel was well enough to be released from the hospital, but far from capable of taking care of himself. Chloe and Wyatt had cut their trip short to come back home, and when Anna drove Miguel back to the ranch she waited until they were nearly to the honeymoon house before she sprang the news on him.

"Your parents are back from South America? When? Why did they bother? This was their vacation!"

She frowned at him. "They got in late last night. And I'm not so sure it was exactly a vacation *or* a honeymoon."

"What do you mean by that?"

She glanced across the seat at him. It was wonderful to see him dressed in his jeans and boots again, rather than hospital pajamas. And even though his loose plaid shirt hid the tight binding around his ribs and his face was pale and gaunt, he looked far better than when he'd first entered the emergency room. For as long as she lived, Anna knew she would never forget the terror she'd gone through, thinking he might die.

"I'm beginning to think my parents went away just to give me a dose of responsibility," she said.

He grunted. "And what has it done for you besides ruin your hands? They must have been crazy and I must have been even crazier for allowing you to step foot in the stables.''

She didn't let his comments rile her. Even though Miguel did it in a domineering way, she was beginning to see it was his way of trying to protect her. "My hands aren't ruined. And anyway, my parents came home because Mother knew she was going to have to take over again."

"Why? Because you've had all you can take of ranch life?"

His caustic question took her by surprise. So did his ill humor. She'd expected him to be chipper this morning and happy he was finally going home. Instead, he was like an angry hornet ready to sting anyone in his path. Most of all her.

She sighed inwardly. "No. I haven't had my fill of ranch life. My roots are here at the Bar M," she reminded him, then when he failed to respond, she added, "Mother's taking over the horses again so that I can take care of you."

His head whipped around to face her. "You're what?"

She smiled at his shocked expression. "You heard me."

"Yeah. But I was hoping I heard wrong. I'll be taking care of myself."

Anna rolled her eyes. "Look, Miguel, everyone knows you're a macho man. It isn't going to ruin your image to have a woman see after you for a few days."

Anna in his house, filling it with her presence and memories that he would never be able to erase. He couldn't let it happen.

"I don't need a woman seeing after me!" he

growled. "Besides, Justine told me your manager is wanting you back on tour again."

Anna's lips thinned to a grim line. She wished her aunt hadn't told Miguel anything about her job. Her piano career already stood like a wall between them. And the more she tried to convince him she wanted to give it up, the more fickle and confused he believed she was.

"Not just yet. I've got time enough to see you back to your feet, cowboy."

He glowered at her. "I can walk to the kitchen. What the hell do I need you around for?"

She tried to tell herself he was a wounded male lashing out because of his condition, rather than at her. But the question hurt just the same. Because there was a deep fear inside Anna that he might not truly need her or want her around.

"To have someone to yell at I suppose," she said quietly.

He glanced at her rigid profile, then groaned out loud. "Damn it, Anna, you know I didn't mean that like it sounded."

She brought the pickup to a halt in front of the honeymoon house, then set the emergency brake. Turning in the seat to face him, she asked, "Do I, Miguel?"

To her surprise he reached over and took her hand. She melted as his long fingers entwined with hers.

"Anna," he said huskily. "It will be— I don't think we should be alone together up here."

"Why? I won't try to ravish you," she promised, and he groaned as her lips tilted up in a teasing little smile.

"Be serious."

"You told me I didn't have a sense of humor. I'm trying to work on it."

Seeing he was getting nowhere with her, he looked away and swiped both hands through his disheveled hair. "I feel naked without my hat."

"The stallion stomped it," she informed him. "It's going to need reshaping."

And if Anna stayed here with him for any length of time, he was going to need reshaping, he thought desperately. But he couldn't send her back down to the ranch. Chloe and Wyatt would be insulted. Anna would be hurt. And he would be lost without her.

This past week she'd sat in the hospital room with him nearly twenty-four hours a day. He hadn't asked for such devotion. She'd simply given it to him. And he'd been unable to send her away. He still couldn't. Miguel knew his weakness now would eventually cost him dearly.

He glanced back at her, and his heart turned over at the yearning he saw on her face. "Anna, don't expect me to be nice while you're here. I'm not necessarily a nice man."

A faint smile touched her lips. "If I need to get away from you, I know how to drive back down the mountain."

He let out a long breath and reached to open the door. "Yeah," he muttered. "I guess you do."

Miguel was bombarded with company over the next several days. The ranch hands, her family, several neighbors, then more of her family all came to wish him a speedy recovery.

Anna could see how their outpouring of concern touched him, but the excitement had also worn him out. He went to bed early and didn't wake until she carried a cup of coffee in to him the next morning.

"What are you doing in my bedroom?" he demanded, jerking the sheet up to his armpits.

Anna smiled at his show of modesty. "Spoiling you. But don't look so worried. I'm not planning on making a habit of it."

He propped himself against the varnished pine headboard and took the steaming cup she offered him. As he sipped, his dark gaze drifted over her slender figure. She was wearing a simple cotton dress printed with tiny yellow daisies. Her hair was loose and waving around her shoulders like a cloud of red silk. He'd never woken to a more beautiful sight.

"This is good," he said with surprise.

She pulled a face at him. "What did you expect, melted tar?"

Before he could reply, she eased down on the side of the bed and studied him as he sipped his coffee.

Her nearness jolted his senses. Her gaze was like fingers softly touching his face and throat and shoulders. "Why are you looking at me in such a way?"

Faint color touched her cheeks. "Just making sure you're all right."

He stared awkwardly down into his coffee cup. "Of course I'm all right," he said gruffly. "There's no need for you to hover over me like a mother hen!"

"Why? Does it make you nervous?"

His gaze swiftly lifted to her face. "It should make *you* nervous, Anna."

She laughed softly, and he could only think how

different she was from the woman he'd first met in the stables several weeks ago. And this Anna, the one he had come to know, was the one he couldn't resist.

"Even if you wanted to make love to me, you couldn't," she said boldly.

His brows shot upward, then his eyes narrowed shrewdly as they scanned her flushed cheeks. "You've never made love to a man. How do you know I can't?"

Her cheeks flamed even brighter. "Because I— you're in a weakened condition. And the binding on your ribs barely allows you to move."

His lips twisted wryly, and then he carefully leaned over and placed his coffee on the nightstand beside the bed. "I'm sure we could think of a way."

Anna's heart began to thump out of control as his hand touched her forearm, then slid slowly upward until his fingers found the edge of her sleeveless dress.

"Please don't make fun of me, Miguel," she whispered. "I can take anything from you but that."

His eyes widened and then his nostrils flared as his gaze slid from her face, down her slender throat and on to the faint shadow of cleavage just above the neckline of her dress.

"I wish I *could* laugh, Anna. I wish I could look at you and tell you that I didn't want you. But that would be lying to both of us."

His face and his voice were both solemn, and when his hand left her arm to boldly cup her breast she gasped with both shock and pleasure.

"Do you see why you shouldn't be here with me?" he asked.

It took Anna a moment to realize he was touching

her because he actually wanted to. Because he *had* to. And the realization flooded her with joy.

She leaned closer and cupped his face with her hands. "I wonder," she whispered, "how long it's going to take for you to trust me."

One hand curved against the back of her neck and pulled her head down to his. It was the first time he'd kissed her since his accident, and Anna was hungry for the taste of him.

She grasped his bare shoulders and leaned closer while consciously making an effort to avoid his ribs. But after a moment she forgot all about his injury. There was nothing weak about the way his lips were consuming hers or the bold thrust of his tongue between her teeth.

His desire fueled hers, and she inched forward as her body yearned to touch his, to feel his heat and strength against her. Her hands explored his shoulders and arms, then thrust into his thick hair.

"Anna! Anna! Do you know how much I want you?" he murmured. His hand slipped beneath the hem of her cotton dress and slid up her bare thigh until his fingers reached the edge of her satin panties. "You've never given yourself to a man. And God help me, when you do, I want that man to be me."

She drew in ragged breaths as she pressed her cheek next to his. Her heart was racing, her body on fire. Never had she felt so needy, so wanton, in her life. Yet with Miguel it felt natural and right. He was the man she'd been saving herself for. He was the only man she would ever want or love.

"You want me for the moment," she whispered doubtfully.

"For the moment. For always."

Trembling, she leaned her head back far enough to gaze into his eyes. She found no mockery in the brown depths. Only longing and regret. The sight of the last pricked her eyes and throat with tears.

"But you wish you didn't feel this way," she said huskily.

He groaned at the pain on her face, the ache wrapping itself around his heart. "I wish I could forget who you are. What you are. I wish I could take you into my arms and make love to you without worrying about tomorrow."

"If you love me, tomorrow will take care of itself."

His fingers traced gentle patterns over her cheek as his eyes delved deep into hers. "'Love,'" he said in a low, mocking voice. "I'm not so sure there is such a thing or if I could ever feel it."

She shook her head ever so slightly. "What about your son? Surely you love him."

His features lost all expression except for his eyes, and they hardened on hers. "I told you I don't want to talk about Carlos. So don't try to bring him into this!"

She refused to give in to him. "Why? I want to be a part of your life!"

He shook his head and muttered a Spanish curse word under his breath. "These days you've spent on the ranch have blinded you. You've conveniently forgotten you have a career—"

Before he could get the rest out, Anna jumped to her feet and stared down at him, her fists clenched at her sides. "You're determined to use my career as a shield! You don't want to own up to the fact that you're just too damn scared to love me!''

In the blink of an eye he grabbed her by the wrist and jerked her back down on the bed beside him. The mattress bounced wildly.

"Miguel!" she practically shouted. "Your ribs!"

"Forget my damn ribs! You asked for this fight. Now you've got it!"

His fingers slipped inside the front of her neckline and jerked her forward. Anna's hands landed against his shoulders with a thud, and she stiffened her arms to keep herself at bay.

"I don't want a fight!" she said with a gasp. "I want you to take a good look at yourself. You are the one who's blinded! Not me!"

A mocking laugh passed his lips. "No. *You* are the one who needs to open your eyes, Anna. I am a wounded man. And I'm not talking about this," he gestured to the binding around his chest. "But inside, where I feel and think, there's nothing but scars. Scars that a woman put there! Maybe I am a coward for not being able to love you. But I like to think I'm simply not being a fool."

Tears filled her eyes and spilled onto her cheeks. "I'm not the woman who hurt you! I would never hurt you! If you can't see that by now...I don't think you ever will."

The sight of her tears was like a lance in Miguel's chest. She was a soft, beautiful angel. To make her cry was a sin in itself. But he had to be cruel to be good to her. She didn't realize that now. But she would someday, he thought sadly.

Groaning with self-derision he reached up and

gently wiped at the drops of pain sliding down her cheeks. "Anna," he said gently, "I understand you would never intentionally hurt me. Right now you think we could be married and the rest of our lives would be bliss. But it wouldn't be that way. We're too different. Our lives are nothing alike."

"If you're talking about my career—"

"Of course I'm talking about it! And I have to be honest with you, Anna. I'm a selfish man. If you were my wife I would want you here with me. Not running off to play for crowds of people! And you would grow to resent my possessiveness."

She shook her head. "I don't want to play for crowds of people."

"That's what you believe." His eyes softened and his hand slid gently up and down her bare, slender arm. "But you're young. Right now your heart and your body are making war with your thinking. But later you'll know what's best for you, and it won't be me."

With a heavy sigh she rose from the bed and walked over to the double windows overlooking the rugged cliff of mountain at the back of the house. This land was like him, she thought. Rough, unyielding, yet terribly beautiful.

Another rush of tears burned her eyes, but he couldn't see them as she kept her gaze on the landscape beyond the window. "What makes you think you know all this, Miguel? Do you have some inner vision?"

She heard the mattress creak and then she felt his warm breath against her ear. His hands curved over her shoulder and she blushed as she felt his bare legs brush against hers. He hadn't bothered to pull a pair of jeans over his boxer shorts. It was an erotic temptation to turn and look at him.

"I'm much older than you, Anna."

"Years don't always equal wisdom," she said softly, then turned and curled her arms around his neck, pressed herself gently against the hard-muscled length of him. "When you lost your son, you gave up on life. You gave up on the notion that you could ever be happy again. But we could be happy, Miguel. We could have children of our own, and we could include Carlos in our family, too."

"Carlos has his own family now."

"But *you* are his father. He needs you."

He pulled back his head and looked at her. "That's only what your grand romantic notions are telling you. But in truth, Carlos has everything he needs. A rich home, the best private school, a mother and stepfather. No, he doesn't need me interfering in his life."

She opened her mouth to argue, but he suddenly pulled out of her embrace, and she watched him pluck a pair of jeans from the end of the bed and quickly pull them on. He was growing much stronger with each passing day. Soon he wouldn't need her care anymore.

She was thrilled he was mending so quickly. But she dreaded the day when he would tell her she had to leave. Until then she had to think of something to open his eyes. To make him see they belonged together.

As Miguel reached for his shirt, he glanced over his shoulder at her. Hunger was on her face as she stood there by the window watching him dress. And it was all he could do to keep from going to her, taking her by the hand, and leading her to his bed.

The struggle within him made his voice gruff when he spoke. "Have you cooked breakfast?"

"Yes." She crossed the room and helped him pull a clean chambray shirt up over his shoulders, then slowly, one by one, she fastened the buttons for him.

When she finished he lifted both of her hands to his lips and kissed the backs of her fingers. She closed her eyes and savored the sweetness of his tender caress.

"Then it's time we ate and got back to our senses," he said.

Anna followed him to the kitchen, but as they sat at the table eating *huevos rancheros*, her mind drifted back to the bedroom and the taste of his lips, the feel of his hand on her breast and thigh. And when she looked across the table at him, his dark eyes told her his thoughts were there, too.

Chapter Nine

"You love him. I can see it on your face. Hear it in your voice each time you mention his name," Chloe said to her daughter. "So what are you going to do about it?"

Anna and her mother were sitting on the front deck of Miguel's house, soaking up the last rays of evening sun. Throughout most of their trivial conversation Anna had been staring off into space, her chin propped on her fist. Now her head jerked up, and she looked around at the older woman in stunned disbelief.

"How could you know—"

Chloe's soft laugh interrupted her. "I'm your mother, darling. When you have children of your own, you'll understand what I mean."

Anna groaned and thrust a hand through her disheveled hair. The past few days she'd spent here with Miguel had been both heaven and hell. Being close to him was too sweet for words. Yet being with him and knowing it would all soon end was ripping her apart. She was no closer to making him see reason than she'd been a week ago. Two weeks ago!

"It looks as though I'll never have children, Mother. Miguel doesn't want anything to do with me," she said grimly. "And I can't see myself with any man but him."

Chloe drummed her fingers thoughtfully on the arm of the lawn chair. "Before your daddy and I left for South America you told me he'd kissed you. That doesn't sound like a man who's not interested."

Anna sighed wearily. "Oh, Mother, Miguel has kissed me many times. It doesn't mean anything to him."

Chloe's brows arched. "Really? Several times? Well, I never took him for a shallow man."

"He isn't!"

Chloe made an open-handed gesture. "You just told me there was nothing behind his kisses."

"Well, there is, but Miguel—" She stopped and groaned with frustration. "Oh, you just don't understand. He doesn't trust women. Least of all me."

"Why least of all you? You told him about Scott, and he thinks you're just on the rebound?"

"He knows about my broken engagement. But that's not the real problem with Miguel. His ex-wife was…well, she apparently came from a monied, well-to-do family in Albuquerque. She was spoiled and self-centered and never took their marriage seriously. She didn't even want their child until after she'd given birth. And then she divorced Miguel and took their son with her. At first he fought for custody, but then he finally decided he couldn't win against their money and power. He had to let his baby go."

"How terribly awful."

"Yes. And he's afraid I'll do the same thing to him."

"Anna! He couldn't believe that of you. You could never inflict that sort of pain on anyone."

Anna got to her feet and began to pace across the redwood deck. Chloe followed her movements with worried eyes.

"He doesn't think I'll do the same thing exactly," Anna told her. "But he does believe I'm too young to know what I want or maybe too emotionally unstable," she added bitterly.

Anna clucked her tongue and shook her head. "You're not thinking of Belinda now?"

Anna glanced guiltily at her mother. "Sometimes I can't help it. I had very bad judgment concerning Scott. And for the past year I've been a strung-out mess. I couldn't eat or sleep."

"You'd been going through a difficult time with your personal life and keeping up with your career. That doesn't mean you're anything like your birth mother! She was on drugs for heaven's sake!"

"I know," Anna miserably agreed. "But look at me now. I'm not much better. I've let myself fall in love with a man who wants nothing to do with me!"

"A person doesn't *let* herself fall in love, honey. It happens, and there is no control over it. That doesn't mean you're unstable, or anything like Belinda. I like to think your daddy and I raised you better."

Anna cast her a wan smile. "You did. I'm just feeling...desperate, I guess. Sometimes I think Miguel does care about me. But he believes my music will eventually pull me away from him. And he doesn't want to take the chance."

"And what about your music, Anna? You'd be giving up so much, years of training—to stay here and be Miguel's wife."

Anna walked over to her mother's chair and faced the older woman head-on. "What would you and Daddy think if I did give up my music?"

"It's not—" She stopped herself, then as she studied Anna's face, a wide smile began to spread across her lips. "You do really know what you want, don't you? It's beyond what your daddy and I think. Your heart has already decided."

Anna sank down on her knees and pressed her mother's hand between her two. Smaller bandages were still taped to her palms where the lariat rope had cut the deepest, but there would be no permanent damage. If she wanted to continue her career at the piano there would be nothing to stop her. Except her heart, she thought. It just wasn't there anymore. It was with Miguel.

"Mother, with Scott I was so naive. I had this notion I could continue to play the piano, be his wife and eventually have children. Everything in its proper place and order. I thought I could keep everybody happy by doing it all. I was so foolish. But falling in love with Miguel has made me see what's really important."

Chloe smiled with gentle understanding. "Somehow I thought Miguel might have that sort of effect on you."

Anna made a face at her. "That's why you and Daddy deliberately stayed away, isn't it? You purposely wanted us to be alone."

Chloe looked terribly guilty. "Well, we didn't think it would hurt anything to give you two a nudge toward each other. And we certainly enjoyed our time away together. But don't you think you should be telling Miguel all of this instead of me? If he knows how certain you are—''

Anna threw up her hands and rose to her feet. ''I've already told him. He's determined I'm headed back to Chicago or New York or any city with a big band or symphony orchestra!'' She walked to the edge of the deck, then turned and headed back to Chloe. ''Telling Miguel how I feel just isn't enough, Mother. I've got to show him. And I don't know how.''

She took a seat again in the lawn chair, then cast her mother a calculated glance. ''Do you know anything about Miguel's son?''

''Not much. He's mentioned him to us a few times. That's all.''

''Does he never see him?''

Chloe's head swung soberly back and forth. ''No. The boy lives in Texas, and Miguel used to go there to see him on occasion. That was when Carlos was much younger. But eventually the visits grew further apart and he quit going altogether. I think it hurt him too much to see the boy being fathered by another man. And Miguel has never believed he had anything to offer the boy that he didn't already have.''

''That's ridiculous.''

''I agree. But oddly enough he's staying away from the boy out of love.''

''That was my same conclusion,'' Anna said, then lapsed into thoughtful silence.

''I could contact Miguel's sister in Colorado and get the child's address. If you wanted it,'' Chloe added.

Anna looked dubiously at her mother. ''Miguel would probably be furious.''

"Or grateful."

Anna sighed. "I only want him to be happy."

The sound of a motor had Chloe suddenly turning her head. She peered at the truck easing up the steep driveway. "Then I guess you're not a bit interested in this visitor," she said smugly.

At the sound of the approaching vehicle, Miguel tossed aside the newspaper and glanced out the window. What in hell was Dalton doing at his house? he wondered, then muttered another curse under his breath as he watched the young vet climb the steps and join the two women on the deck.

His business was down at the barns. Not here! If it wasn't for Chloe, he'd go out there and tell the man to get back in his truck and make tracks. But she used his services from time to time, and anyway he had no right to dictate who Anna talked to.

Yet, as the long minutes ticked away and the doctor continued to linger, his blood began to boil. By the time Dalton finally left and Chloe followed him down the mountain in her own vehicle, Miguel was ready to eat nails.

When Anna came back into the house, he met her at the door. "Did you have a nice visit with the young doctor?"

She grimaced at the sarcasm in his voice. He'd been testy the past two days, but nothing like this. And because at this moment she needed him to be exactly the opposite, she lashed back at him.

"Not hardly! He wasn't here to see me. He came to tell Mother the horse's foot is sound again and she can resume running him."

She stepped around him and started toward the kitchen. He followed on her heels. "That took you less than a minute to give me that information. Dalton was out there for thirty!"

Her brows arched haughtily as she glanced over her shoulder at him. "You were counting?"

"Don't sass me!"

She whirled on him. "You really have some gall, Miguel! You tell me you can't have anything to do with me and then act outraged if I talk to another man! You're behaving like a...crazy man!"

Was it any wonder, Miguel thought wildly. Each time he looked at her, he wanted her. He had to constantly fight with himself to keep a safe distance away from her, and the effort was shredding his nerves.

He grasped her by the arm, and she gasped as his fingers bit into her flesh. "What do you expect from me, Anna? I'm human. I can only take so much!"

"Why don't you try turning that around, Miguel. Just how much rejection do you think I can take from you? Maybe the next time the doctor asks me out, I'll go!"

His dark eyes were suddenly blazing. "He asked you out!"

Anna wasn't going to lie just to soothe his temper. Besides, she thought angrily, he needed to see the truth. He refused to open his eyes or his heart. Refused to trust her love.

"To the movies."

"The bastard!"

"And what are you, Miguel? At least he isn't pretending."

Miguel couldn't bear it. The feelings inside him were so raw, so achingly full for her he couldn't stand to have them labeled as phony.

"You think I'm pretending?" he said through clenched teeth.

Her gaze was unwavering on his. "You're not being completely honest."

His eyes clashed with hers a few moments longer, and then without any warning his arms were around her, dragging her next to him.

"Why do you do this to me?" he whispered roughly against her lips. "Why do you make me love you?"

"You don't love me," she said hollowly.

His hands clamped the sides of her waist, crushed her hips against his. Anna felt every inch of her body begin to sizzle as the bulge of his desire told her exactly what he wanted.

"What do you know about it, Anna?" he demanded in a low growl. "You're still a virgin."

"That isn't a crime! Sex and love are two different things."

His lips twisted cruelly. "And how could you know? Maybe we should see just how much you want to love me!"

Her mouth opened to speak, but his lips suddenly captured hers, blotting out anything she might have said. She groaned a protest in the back of her throat and tried to push herself away.

Miguel's hands left her waist, circled around her shoulders and drew her tightly to him. Instantly the strength and warmth of his body enveloped her senses, the rough search of his lips drew her into a dark velvety place where only pleasure existed.

She opened her mouth, accepted the probing search of his tongue. And then she was lost as the taste of

him overwhelmed her. Nothing mattered except that
he go on holding her, kissing her.

They were halfway down the hallway before Anna
realized she'd moved anywhere. At the door of his
bedroom, he propelled her backward. One step, two,
five and ten. Then the back of her legs hit the side of
the bed.

The jolt finally broke the contact of their lips, and
she would have toppled sideways if Miguel's hands
hadn't closed around her rib cage. He tossed her back
onto the mattress, and she landed with a bounce.

For a moment sanity tried to swim through the thick
desire muddling her mind. "Miguel, you're going to
tear your ribs apart!"

He planted his fists on either side of her head as he
leaned over her and gazed down at her face. "Right
now I don't care if I ever breathe again."

The rough passion in his voice was as erotic as the
touch of his hand. Anna could not resist it or the longing on his face. With a groan she brought her arms up
and around his neck, pulled him down to her.

His warm lips savored the soft skin beneath her ear,
then kissed the throb of her heart where it pulsed
wildly at the base of her throat. Her body arched
against him, silently begging him closer.

His fingers fumbled urgently with the buttons on her
silk blouse, then finally the fabric fell away to expose
pale plump breasts spilling over pale pink lace. The
sight caused Miguel's rough intake of breath, then
with a self-deriding groan he lowered his head and
buried his face between the soft mounds.

Anna's legs wrapped around his, her fingers buried
themselves in his hair and pressed against his scalp.
With slow, exquisite torture his mouth moved over her

silky skin until the barrier of her flimsy bra stopped his downward progress.

Quickly he reached beneath her and unfastened the clasp, then pushed the offending garment up and out of his way. The beautiful sight of her caused his breath to quicken, his eyes to light with inner fire. Her nipples were pink rosebuds just waiting for his mouth to bring them to full blossom. And he couldn't deny himself or her.

By the time he lifted his head and nuzzled his cheek to hers, Anna was panting, gripping his shoulders with a need that was consuming her.

"I do want to love you, Miguel. Not with just my body but with every part of me. What else can I say, what can I do to make you believe me?"

Love him. *Love him!* No, it was too wonderful to be true. He couldn't let himself believe, even for a few moments, that what she felt for him would always last. It was a risk his scarred heart just couldn't take.

Slowly his head lifted, and his eyes were grave as he looked down at her. Her features were full of misery, and it cut Miguel deeply to think he was hurting her, that what he felt for her was actually causing her anguish. But it had to be this way, he told himself. Otherwise they were both bound for far worse grief.

He pushed himself away from her, wincing as the tenderness in his ribs joined the ache in his heart. "There is nothing you can do. Right now—" He stopped, turned his back to her and drew in a heavy breath. "I want you to pack your things and go back to the ranch house."

"No!"

He whirled around. "Then I'll do it for you! Because you can't stay here another night!"

"Why? Because of what nearly happened just now?"

With a muttered oath he stepped back to the bed and jerked the sides of her blouse across her naked breasts. "It would have been a mistake, Anna," he said flatly.

His words ripped through her like shards of broken glass. "Mistake! Did that feel like a mistake to you?"

"A drink of tequila is pleasurable, too. But that doesn't necessarily mean it's good for you."

Unmindful of her half-dressed state, she jumped to her feet. "You're coarse and hateful! And if you didn't have broken ribs I'd take great pleasure in slapping your face!"

"Don't let my broken ribs stop you," he snarled.

Fury whipped her hand back, but she didn't follow through on his invitation. As she looked into his rigid face, it dawned on her that he was deliberately provoking her. He wanted to anger her, to drive her away so there would be no chance of him making love to her.

Her hand fell limply at her side, and she closed her eyes and breathed deeply as she tried to calm her racing thoughts. If he was that desperate to get her out of here there would be no use in her staying. She couldn't make him love her, and for her to try to force him to have the sort of feelings she needed from him would only be demeaning to both of them.

"What's the matter," he sneered. "Afraid you'll really hurt me?"

She quickly turned away from him and buttoned her blouse with shaking fingers.

"No. I've decided you're right. You don't want me here and I'm not…going to impose myself on you any longer. You can obviously take care of yourself. You certainly don't need the aggravation I'm causing you."

Not daring to look at him, she hurried out of the room. In her own bedroom, she began to throw her things into a canvas duffel bag. Tears were rolling down her face when she heard his soft knock on the side of the open door.

Her hands paused in their task, but she refused to turn and face him. The pain of looking on his face right now would simply be too great.

"Where are you going?" he asked quietly.

She swallowed and hoped her voice wouldn't belie her tears. "Back to the ranch house. Not that it's any of your business."

"You're right. It isn't."

There was nothing more she could say, and after a moment she heard his footsteps move away.

Once Anna knew he was truly out of sight, she sank down on the side of the bed, covered her face with her bandaged hands and burst into sobs.

A little more than a week later Anna walked into the study, tossed her purse on the chesterfield couch and flopped wearily down beside it. A few feet away at a large oak desk, Chloe looked up from her paperwork and peered over the tops of her reading glasses.

"Did you get the doctor paid?"

Anna groaned. She didn't know why her mother had sent her on such a useless errand. She could have waited on a statement from Dr. Dalton and sent him a check in the mail. But she'd insisted on getting the bill taken care of immediately.

"Don't call that man a doctor. I think Miguel was

right about him. He thinks he's a Romeo disguised as a veterinarian. And he's not good at either profession.''

Chloe struggled not to smile. ''What's the matter? Did he ask you out again?''

''And again! I could hardly get away from the man.''

''You should be flattered. He's considered a catch around these parts. Why don't you go out with him?''

Anna grimaced. ''Because I'm not interested in him.''

''Well, you don't have to be interested just to get out and enjoy dinner or a movie.''

''I'd be miserable.''

Chloe sighed. ''And what are you now? I can't remember the last time I saw a smile on your face.''

Anna pressed her fingers against her throbbing temples. The effort to ward off the veterinarian's advances without being rude had worn on her already-frazzled nerves. As Dalton had flirted, all Anna had been able to think about was Miguel. His scent, his touch, the sheer pleasure it gave her just to be near him. No man could ever take his place.

''I know. I came home to get my bearings straight and look at me,'' she said with self-disgust. ''I didn't know what pain was until Miguel got ahold of me.''

Chloe pulled off her glasses and laid them on her desk, then, folding her hands together, she leveled a stern look on her daughter. ''Then why don't you drive up to the honeymoon house and talk to him again. It's been a week since you left. You haven't seen him since. Maybe he's changed his mind about things.''

Anna shot her mother a dry look. "If that's the case, why hasn't he let me in on it?"

"The man can't drive," Chloe reasoned.

"He has a cellular. All he has to do is pick it up and call me." But he hadn't even done that much, she thought miserably.

"You're right," Chloe was forced to agree. Then, drumming her fingers on the desktop, she said, "Then go out with Dalton. That should wake Miguel up!"

Anna left her seat on the couch. At her mother's desk, she propped her hip on one corner. "I don't want him to come to me out of jealousy. I'd never do that to him!"

"Then you'll have to think of something else to make him sit up and take notice."

Anna tilted her head back and stared desperately at the ceiling. "What would you do? What did you do when you fell in love with Daddy?"

"Well, it was the other way around with us, Anna. I was the reluctant one. I was scared to death because Wyatt was so different from me. He'd always lived in Houston, and I was certain he'd wind up leaving me after a few months."

Desperate hope flickered in Anna's eyes as her gaze whipped back to her mother's. "That's the same way Miguel feels about me! So what made you finally realize things would work?"

Chloe smiled with fond remembrance. "I guess when I saw what great lengths Wyatt would take just to make me happy, I decided he must really, really love me."

Anna grew silent and thoughtful as she considered her mother's words. After a few moments Chloe left her seat and walked around the desk. Taking her daughter's hand she asked, "What are you thinking, darling? What are you going to do?"

Anna lifted her head and gave her mother a shaky smile. "I'm going to Texas. And if by some wild chance Miguel asks about me, don't tell him anything about where I've gone."

Light work. What the hell was light work on a ranch? Miguel wondered. There was no such thing, and he'd told the doctor so. But the man hadn't relented. He'd insisted Miguel needed at least one more week before he could do anything strenuous.

Miguel was just thankful the doc had given him the okay to drive again. He hadn't expected that being confined to the house for a few days would be such a hard thing to endure. But after Anna had left, his days had been nothing but pure hell. He'd tried to read, watch TV, listen to the radio, but all he'd ended up doing was staring at the walls thinking about her.

He missed her more than he would his own arm or leg, and he'd fought with himself to keep from calling her. Mainly because he was afraid she would come back to him and then he'd have to go through her leaving all over again.

It was better to forget her now, he told himself. Once she realized there was no chance for them to be together, she'd go back to her career. Where she belonged.

The ranch yard was unusually quiet when he pulled his Explorer to a halt and climbed out. As he looked around at the pens and barns and worksheds, he realized just how much he'd missed his work. A cowboy could stand a roof over his head for so long, and then he had to get back beneath the sky.

The pen of working ponies was empty, and the hands were nowhere to be found. They must be moving cattle, he decided, then jamming his hands in the pockets of his jeans he glanced at the stables across the way.

He wasn't sure he could handle running into Anna just now. But he figured Chloe was inside the building and he needed to speak with her. She would want to know the results of his checkup and how soon it would be before he could get back to work full-time and Harlan could go back to seeing after his own ranch.

The stables were quiet, too. Miguel ran into the two cowhands he'd forced into becoming grooms and they both greeted him warmly.

"Mrs. Sanders says we're bonafide grooms now," one of them said proudly.

"Yeah," the other one added, "nothin' could make us go back to brandin' calves. The next race Mrs. Sanders wins, we're gonna be right there in the winner's circle with her."

"So you're getting the hang of things now?"

They nodded in unison. "We're real glad you put us here, Mr. Chavez. And we're real glad you're up and about now."

Miguel thanked them both, then peered farther on down the long building. "Is Mrs. Sanders anywhere around?"

"Down in the tack room."

Miguel nodded then quickly headed to find her. He half expected to run into Anna somewhere along the way, but she was nowhere in sight. She'd probably decided, now that her mother was back, there was no need for her to deal with temperamental horses, dirty stalls and heavy feed buckets.

"Miguel! How wonderful to see you!" Chloe exclaimed when he stepped into the tack room. She tossed the bit and bridle to one side and went to give him a brief hug. "We've missed you terribly around here."

He smiled sheepishly. "I'm sorry I've put a strain on things. But the doctor says I can begin regular work next week."

"I'm glad. Not just to have my foreman back, but glad you're doing so well. You had us all very worried for a while. And Emily and Cooper will never forget that you saved little Harlan. None of us will."

His gaze dropped to the toes of his boots. "You're all making too much of that." He looked back up at her. "Where's all the hands? I came down to say hello and couldn't find any of them."

"Moving cattle. The south section has gotten pretty well grazed out."

He nodded, then glanced awkwardly around the room. "Uh...how's Anna? Isn't she helping you with the horses?"

Chloe folded her arms across her chest. "No. Anna's gone. She left a few days ago."

Stunned, he stared at her. "Gone! Where?" Then before she could answer, he nodded knowingly. "Back to her career."

Chloe shook her head. "I don't think Anna has a piano career anymore. She told her manager she was finished. She wasn't going back."

Miguel swore under his breath. "The fool girl! Doesn't she realize what she's throwing away?"

"Money and fame don't always equal happiness, Miguel. And that's what Wyatt and I want for our daughter. Whether it's making music or having a passel of kids, it's her choice.''

A bunch of kids, Miguel's thoughts echoed. When he'd talked to Anna about his son, Carlos, she'd told him they could have children of their own. But he'd rejected the idea. Rejected her. He'd more or less told her to go out and have her babies with someone else!

"If Anna hasn't gone back to playing the piano, where did she go?"

Chloe quickly glanced away from him. "Uh…well, I'm not sure. Ruidoso probably. She didn't say exactly where."

Miguel frowned at her evasive answer. "Didn't say? You mean you let her leave and you didn't even know where she was going!"

Chloe shrugged. "She's a grown woman, and she wanted some time to herself. She doesn't have to answer to her parents anymore. And—" she looked at him pointedly "—you weren't interested."

Interested! His every waking moment was spent on her. He wanted her to be happy and safe. He wanted only the best for her. He *loved* her!

"She's left with Dalton! That's why you don't want to tell me!"

Chloe made a complacent gesture with her hands. "I don't know about that. He has been pestering her to go out with him. Maybe she decided a few days away with him would lift her spirits."

He whipped his hat off his head and whacked it against his leg. "Are you crazy, Chloe! You know what that damn man is! He'll only use her, then throw her away when he gets tired of her."

Chloe decided it was time for her to dig back into the stack of bridles. Turning her back to Miguel she said as casually as she could manage, "Anna has to grow up and learn these things for herself sometimes. If she gets hurt...well, you know as well as I, Miguel, that's just part of life."

Her remark tore another curse from Miguel, and he slapped his hat back on his head.

"*You* might look at it that way, Chloe, but I can't. I'm going after her. I'm not about to let that ba—jerk, lay his hands on her! And if he already has I'll kill him!"

His boots clattered on the wooden floor as he headed out the door. Chloe whirled around to call him back. "Miguel! Wait!"

She raced out of the room and caught up to him halfway down the building.

Miguel kept on walking. "Don't try to stop me, Chloe. You can't."

"But you don't know where she is," Chloe reasoned as she stumbled to keep up with him.

"I'll start with Dalton's secretary. She'll know where he is."

"But—Miguel, I'm expecting her back any time today! In fact, she promised to call this evening if she couldn't make it. So why don't you go home, and I'll let you know the minute I hear from her."

Miguel glanced at his watch. "It's four already. I'm going to go pack a few things. If she hasn't called by five I'm leaving."

Chloe nodded, then silently prayed, for everyone's sake, that Anna showed up soon.

Back at the honeymoon house, Miguel jammed a few pieces of clothing into a duffel bag, then paced mindlessly from room to room.

If Anna was with Dalton, he'd never forgive himself. He'd hurt her by sending her away. And she was so young and innocent she might just turn to him for comfort.

So what's your problem? a nasty voice growled inside his head. You weren't willing to pledge your love, your life to her. You gave her up because you were scared of loving, losing and giving up another child born from your own flesh.

Groaning aloud with torment, he walked out to the back of the house and stared up at the wild cliff towering up toward the even higher grove of pines. Anna loved the cliff. And this ranch. She'd come back here for solace, because it was her home, her deepest roots. But he'd mocked her idea to stay here. He'd been afraid to believe she would actually consider staying. And even more afraid that if she did stay he could not help but fall in love with her.

But that had happened, anyway. Now she was gone. He'd probably lost her. If not to Dalton, then to his own stubborn refusal to accept her into his life.

"Miguel! Miguel! Are you here?"

His head whipped around. That was Anna's voice!

Quickly he rounded the house, then stopped dead in his tracks. Anna was standing on the deck, and her arm was around a boy. A dark-headed boy who looked amazingly like himself.

"Carlos!"

At the sound of his name, the boy stepped forward and looked expectantly, hopefully at his father.

Miguel opened his arms, and he was certain a choir of angels began to sing above his head as Carlos ran straight to him and flung his arms around his waist.

Too choked for words, Miguel could say nothing. He held his child tightly, patted his back and ruffled his hair until the tears in his throat eased enough to speak.

"Carlos, how did you get here?"

The boy smiled tentatively over his shoulder at Anna, who was waiting quietly on the deck. "Anna brought me. She's very nice." He looked back up at his father. "At first I didn't want to come. I was afraid you'd be mad. But she talked me into coming."

"Mad! Why would I be angry?"

Carlos's chin fell against his chest. "I didn't think you wanted to see me. You quit writing and never come to Texas to see me anymore," he mumbled.

Miguel wedged his forefinger beneath Carlos's chin and lifted his face. "Oh, *chico,* that wasn't because I didn't want to see you. I thought it would be better if I didn't interfere in your life. I didn't think you needed me."

The boy shook his head. "You're my father," he said as if that were the most precious thing on earth to him.

Miguel could only tug him back against his chest and hold him close. Later he would explain to his son just how much he loved and needed him. But for now it was enough to be able to simply touch him.

Leaving the deck, Anna slowly approached the two of them and waited a few steps away. Eventually Miguel lifted his head, and the moment her eyes met his, her heart soared to heaven. Everything was going to be all right. He would never send her away again.

"You did this for me," he said in an awed voice. "How did you know where to find him?"

"Your sister."

He swallowed, then, straightening, he tucked Carlos

beneath his arm, and the two of them stepped over to her.

"I was afraid you'd left with Dalton," he told her.

Anna groaned. "Mother is going to pay for that, believe me."

A grin suddenly split his face, and he shook his head. "No. I'm glad for her misdeed. It made me see how foolish I was to let any man have the chance to win your love."

"That will never happen, Miguel."

He reached for her hand, squeezed it, then tugged her into the circle of his other arm. "You will marry me?"

"On one condition," she said, then smiled down at Carlos.

"Anything," he agreed. "Life would be hell without you. I know that now."

"My one condition is that Carlos is included in our family, too."

"It'll never be any other way," he promised, then glanced at his son. "What do you think?"

Carlos grinned. "I think you should kiss her and make it official!"

Miguel chuckled. "I think you're absolutely right," he said. Then, turning his head to Anna, he kissed her with love and hope and happiness.

The space beside him was empty, the sheet cold. Miguel sat up in bed and glanced around the room. She was nowhere in sight.

He threw back the covers and pulled on a pair of jeans. And then he spotted her. Through a long, open window, he could see her standing on the beach. The morning sun was just breaking over the horizon, spilling glorious pinks, yellows and magenta through the sky and over the water. The vibrant colors silhouetted her slender figure in dark blue silk.

The flimsy garment fluttered around her bare legs and molded against her curves. Her long, flaming hair lay loose and wild against her back.

The precious sight of his wife squeezed his heart and filled him with such tender emotion that he could only gaze and wonder how such happiness had come to him.

Then finally he was compelled to leave the house and join her. The sound of his approach was drowned out by the ocean rolling up on the sand. When his arms slid around her waist from the back, she squealed with pleasurable shock.

"Miguel! I thought you were asleep!"

He pushed her wind-tangled hair away from the back of her neck, then planted a warm kiss on her nape.

"How do you expect me to sleep without your body next to mine?"

She laughed softly and spread her hands over his strong, brown forearms. "Last night was our wedding night. You haven't had time to get used to having me in bed with you. Yet," she added seductively.

He buried his face in the side of her hair and inhaled the heady scent of gardenia. Last night she'd given herself to him so tenderly, so passionately that just the memory of it turned him inside out. She was his woman in every sense now. And he would never let her go.

"Our wedding," he repeated with a smile in his voice. "I don't think I've ever seen anything more beautiful. With the church full of candles and flowers.

And you all in white. It was so wonderful to have your whole family there."

Anna suddenly giggled. "I still can't believe Adam accidentally caught my bouquet."

Miguel chuckled. "Well, he did instantly toss it to your cousin Caroline."

"Yes. But he believes he's jinxed. If a woman even looks at him crosswise now, he'll probably take off running."

"I hope not. Everyone should be as happy as we are."

Sighing, she turned in his arms and brought her hand up to his face. "You are happy, aren't you?"

His forehead rested against hers. "I didn't know I could ever feel this way. And to have Carlos back in my life, too. I can hardly believe it."

Anna smiled. "He looked very handsome yesterday at the wedding. Just like his father. And I was very glad Charlene came, too. You know, when I talked to her in Texas, she admitted how sorry she was for the way she treated you all those years ago. And I believe she truly is. She seems to want to make amends."

"Yes. Giving me equal custody rights of Carlos made me see that. Now he can live with us during the summer and visit on most of the holidays." He pressed his lips to hers, then whispered, "Thanks to you, *querida*. If you hadn't come into my life I would still be lost and festering with bitterness."

"And if you hadn't come into mine I would still be swearing off all men forever."

"You have sworn off all men. Except this one," he said with a laugh, then swept her up in his arms and started back to the house.

"Miguel! Miguel! Where are we going? I wanted to see the sunrise!"

"We're going to work."

"But this is our honeymoon!" she exclaimed.

"Yes. But Carlos is expecting me to produce him a brother or sister. I can't disappoint him."

She pressed her lips against the side of his neck. "Hmm. If that's the case, then I guess the sunrise can wait."

*   *   *   *   *

Who will lift Adam's jinx? See when he meets his perfect match in the next **TWINS ON THE DOORSTEP** *book, coming from Silhouette Romance early in 1999!*

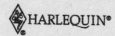